THE SHADOW
GUESTS

Joan Aiken

THE SHADOW GUESTS

JONATHAN CAPE

THIRTY BEDFORD SQUARE LONDON

First published 1980
© 1980 by Joan Aiken Enterprises Ltd

Jonathan Cape Ltd, 30 Bedford Square, London WC1

British Library Cataloguing in Publication Data

Aiken, Joan
The shadow guests.
I. Title
823'.9'1J   PZ7.A2695

ISBN 0-224-01797-7

NOTE

Readers may be interested to know that *Flatland*, referred to in this story, is still in print. Its full title is *Flatland: A Romance of Many Dimensions*, by Edwin A. Abbott (Dover Publications).

Printed in Great Britain by The Anchor Press Ltd
and bound by Wm Brendon & Son Ltd
both of Tiptree, Essex

Chapters

1

Meeting

NOBODY WAS AT THE airport to meet him.

One of the stewardesses had told him there was a place called a Rendezvous Area where you could go and wait if your friends hadn't turned up when the plane landed. So that was where he went. It was next to the Information Desk, a set of plush-covered benches, striped in pink and brown, with a few anxious people sitting on them, gazing about in every direction. But Cosmo preferred to stand, leaning against the trolley that held his luggage – two cases, a carry-on bag, and a tennis racquet.

He stared at the mass of people, streaming up and down the airport concourse, and wondered how he would ever know which one was looking for him.

"Cousin Eunice will probably come to meet you herself," his father had said. "But I suppose she might be giving a lecture or tutoring somebody that day; then she'd have to arrange for someone else to come."

Could any of these women be Cousin Eunice? A fat blonde one with pouches under her eyes: he hoped not. A thin dark one in a corduroy windcheater: she looked nice,

7

but she walked straight past. A younger one—no, but she had a girl of about six with her. Cousin Eunice was not married and had no children.

"Have I met her? Was she there when we visited Uncle Ted that time?"

He remembered the place—most clearly and hauntingly he remembered it—not the house, but the way a fold of hazelwood ran down to the river, and a brook, where he and Mark had built a dam, and a deep dark millpool and a weir, and a footbridge by which you went across to the island where the mill was. A huge field shaped like a half-moon. If anything could cheer him at the moment—but nothing could, really—it would be the prospect of living at Courtoys Mill.

"No, Cousin Eunice wasn't there at that time," his father had said. "She was away at Cambridge, studying." There had been something bitten-back about his voice—the way people talk when they are concealing things considered unsuitable for the young. His father had talked like that most of the time in the last month or two. So—was there something peculiar about Cousin Eunice? Surely not; his father seemed to put a lot of trust in her. "She'll look after you all right, and get you all the stuff you need for school," he had said. "And I'll come to England as soon as I can."

But where was Cousin Eunice now? He shivered, feeling horribly isolated all of a sudden. Thirty hours in the plane was no joke—and then to have nobody meet you—

People were rushing up and down the concourse like lemmings, carrying their luggage or pushing it on trolleys. The loudspeaker added to the frantic atmosphere by a constant stream of urgent appeals.

"This is your last call for Air France flight four-oh-three to Marseilles now at gate seven. Will Mr Panizelos on

Olympic flight nine-nine-two please go *at once* to gate ten. Will Doctor Creasey, recently arrived from Los Angeles on Pan Am three-five-three, please go to the airport information desk. Will the driver meeting Captain Wang Tao Ping please go to the information desk."

A grey-haired man hurried up to the plush benches, and the worried girl with the enormous blue rucksack joyfully jumped up and ran to hug him. Many of the faces that had begun to seem familiar were gone, they were being replaced by others. I have been waiting here longer than anybody else, Cosmo thought. The harried woman, the fat impatient bald man, the girl with the baby had all gone. A new series of waiting, expectant people had replaced them.

Cosmo longed for a huge drink of cold water. The last meal served on the plane had been a disgusting sweet stale sticky bun and a half-cup of lukewarm coffee tasting like liquid that cardboard had been boiled in; it was far from thirst-quenching. But there was no refreshment bar in this part of the airport. Presumably the people who built the place had thought that anybody getting off a plane wouldn't want food or drink; they would just want to hurry away.

Ma had said once that thinking about lemons would help you not to be thirsty. He tried it. But the lemons refused to become real in his mind; instead he heard Ma's voice, laughing, persuasive; and *that* was unfortunate, because a terrible, choking lump swelled in his throat, making the thirst even more of a torment.

A plump woman scurried by, calling, "Bert, Percy, Oscar – come along – hurry up – don't dawdle!" She was pushing a trolley stacked high with massive cases and bundles and duffel-bags – how could she possibly manage it? And how could she possibly have called her children

9

Bert, Percy, and Oscar—three of the ugliest names in the English language?

Cosmo was not particularly fond of his own name, but he did feel it was infinitely better than any of those three. He turned to see if the straggling sons of the fat woman deserved their dismal names, and was obliged to admit that she had chosen suitably. Bert—if Bert was the biggest—slouched sulkily along, the shock of sawdust-coloured hair flopping over his acne'd face not at all concealing its disagreeable expression; he was drinking out of a can of lemonade shandy and didn't offer to help his mother push the luggage-trolley although he was at least a head taller than she; Oscar was a horrible little imp with tight yellow curls and fat cheeks covered in sticky grubbiness from the ice-lolly he was sucking; in his other hand he held a space-man's trident which he poked at the legs of anyone who came near him; Percy, the middle one, was not much better; he had glasses and a peevish expression; he was eating out of a bag of crisps and read a motor-magazine as he walked, taking no notice of his mother's anxious cries. Poor thing, Cosmo thought, fancy having children like that, but it was probably her own fault for the way she'd brought them up.

"Will the driver meeting Mrs Mohammed Ghazni please go to the information desk?"

The arrivals indicator clicked and whirred; his own plane, Sydney to London, which had been up at the top, marked "On time" and "Landed" had been replaced by the flight from San Francisco, sixty minutes late. How would Cousin Eunice know that his flight had arrived? Presumably she would ask at the desk. Then it occurred to him that he himself could have a message broadcast. What should it say? "Will Cousin Eunice Doom, supposed to be meeting Cosmo

Curtoys, please come to the desk?" But if it were not Cousin Eunice who had come to meet him? "Will the friends meeting Cosmo Curtoys—?"

Friends sounded wrong—he had no friends over here, it seemed like presuming on people's good-nature to call them his friends in advance.

He had a sudden horrible vision of Percy, Bert and Oscar, with malevolent looks on their faces, charging up to the information desk where he stood nervously waiting.

"You Cosmo Curtoys? Well, we're here to meet you, but we ain't your *friends*, we can tell you that from the start!"

After a good deal of hesitation he put his problem to the girl at the desk, and she solved it at once.

"Will Miss Eunice Doom, or the person supposed to be meeting Cosmo Curtoys"—she pronounced it wrong, because he had showed her his passport, in spite of the fact that he had clearly said *Curtis*—"please come to the information desk."

Having his name called out like that, even pronounced wrongly, made him feel as if everybody must be staring at him, but of course they were not; they were all far too worried about catching their planes or finding whoever they were supposed to meet; and it did not produce Cousin Eunice either.

"Had she far to come?" the information girl asked.

"I think about eighty miles—from near Oxford."

"Oh well, I'd give her a while yet before you start to worry." And the girl went back to all the other people who were fighting for her attention.

Cosmo began thinking about Cousin Eunice again, trying to remember what he knew about her. Younger than Father, but still quite old, in her thirties. A Professor of Mathematics – that was a bit daunting. Suppose, when he was living with her, that she kept pouncing on him. "Hey, Cosmo, quick – the square root of ninety-three! Multiply eighteen by twenty-four!" But Father said mathematicians didn't think in those terms at all any more – it was all much more stretchy. And the dull jobs like square roots were all done by calculators. Rather a pity, in a way: Cosmo enjoyed, when he was in bed at night, letting numbers make patterns in his mind. Take the three-times table, for instance: it went three-six-nine-two-five-eight-one-four-seven-zero, before starting up again at three; much more interesting than dull old five-times, which just went five-zero-five-zero. But *why* did three-times have ten changes before coming back to base, what governed these patterns? Seven-times had ten changes, six-times had five – but then four-times and eight-times both had five as well, it seemed odd that they weren't all different.

Anyway, back to Cousin Eunice ... a mathematician really ought to be tall and skinny with a long nose and glasses and grey hair scraped back in a knob. Like a wicked governess. But Father had said she wasn't in the least like that. He seemed to find it hard to describe her though – and that was odd, because he had grown up with her, at Courtoys Place, before it was sold to pay death duties. Death duties ... you would think that, once you had died, you had no more duties. *Duties*, to Cosmo, meant hair, teeth, wash face, make bed, put pyjamas away, help with the breakfast dishes ... "Have you boys done your morning duties?" Ma would call, putting on a severe tone. "All right, then you can go out."

But suppose nobody was sure if you *had* died, did you have to pay death duties then?

Lost in thought, he took several minutes to realize that

somebody was standing in front of him, surveying him doubtfully.

"Would you—by any chance—be Cosmo Curtoys?" She gave it the right pronunciation, Curtis.

"Yes—yes, I am."

"My goodness, you're much larger than I expected. I'm sorry I'm late; I had to give a lecture. People *will* ask questions ... Is this all your luggage? No more? Oh, good, then we can be off right away. I don't like to keep Lob waiting; he gets miserable."

She spun the trolley round with a strong hand, thrusting it along in the direction that said "Short Term Car Park". What about me? Cosmo thought somewhat indignantly, following her, doesn't it matter if I'm kept waiting at the end of a thirty-hour flight? but, as if she had heard him thinking, she went on in the same tone, "Humans have resources, they don't ever need to be bored if they learn to use their minds sensibly, but dogs are different."

Oh, so Lob is a dog? Then Cosmo remembered his father saying, "I wonder if the dog is still alive? Old Uncle Ted Doom—Eunice's father—had this St Bernard who was about as big as a pony."

The luggage trolley had an infernal habit of skidding off sideways, refusing to run straight, which was particularly awkward on the steep ramp they now had to descend; Cosmo grabbed the side to push it straight and so got his first good look at his Cousin Eunice—he supposed she must be his Cousin Eunice though she had not said so.

Only about one per cent of his guesses about her had been right. She was tall, with big hands and feet, and her hair pulled back in some kind of elaborate bun at the back of her head, but there was a *lot* of the hair, a bright, fair colour, almost lemony, like evening-primroses, and more of it hung over her eyes in a fringe. Nor did she look very old, it was hard to believe that she was even as much as thirty. He supposed her face was rather plain – a big, wide mouth, straight nose, and two grey eyes which at the moment held an impatient expression. "Why do these blasted things *never* go straight – Ah, that's better – " as they came to ground level, a rather dismal out-of-doors, with a long stretch of pavement, a concrete canopy, and signs saying "Courtesy Buses stop here".

"Now," said Cousin Eunice, "you hang on there and I'll go and get the car. Shan't be a minute; I managed to park on the ground level." A sniff. "Found a slot that said *Airport Manager*; *he* wasn't there, so *I* took it. That's one thing – "

She disappeared in mid-sentence. This, he soon discovered, was a frequent occurrence with Cousin Eunice. Generally it meant that she had had an idea which needed to be worked out on paper immediately. But when she saw you next, no matter how long an interval had elapsed in the meantime, she would go right on with what she had started to say, assuming that you too would remember where she had stopped. Which was comforting, on the whole. Now she was as good as her word, returning almost at once in a huge, stately, battered car.

" – One thing about having a Rolls," she went on, "you can put it almost anywhere and nobody makes a fuss. Now I'll introduce you to Lob – that's the first thing. He was very fond of your father, so I expect he will be prepared to make friends."

Lob had the slightly mournful expression that St Bernards wear. He was sitting in the back of the car, where the ample floor space was just enough to accommodate him comfortably. Cousin Eunice opened the rear door and he

14

extended a front paw, which Cosmo took. It was as thick as a table leg. Lob was black and white and shaggy; he had a sweetish musty smell, and, after a polite moment, removed his paw from Cosmo's grasp with an absent-minded air, as if he could not quite remember how it had got there in the first place.

"He's very old," said Cousin Eunice, opening the boot. "He misses my father a lot; my father died two years ago. That's right, put your racquet on top—good. Now you come in the front by me."

The Rolls smelt overpoweringly of Lob, but Cosmo supposed that, after a bit, he would get used to this. He did ask, though, if he could open the window.

"Of course you can," said Cousin Eunice absently, hunting for her purse to pay the car-park fee. "Have you ten pence by any chance? Oh no, I suppose it's all Australian money. Never mind, he'll have to change a pound. If you look in the glove shelf you'll find a bottle of lemonade—I always feel parched after a long flight."

He had been too rushed—and shy—to suggest stopping to buy a drink, and was impressed by this evidence of thoughtfulness. Lemonade wasn't the best choice—too sweet and fizzy—he'd rather it had been water—but then he discovered that it was home-made lemonade, cool and sour, with bits of cut-up lemon-peel. That brought back Ma for a while, and he was silent as Cousin Eunice manoeuvred the stately car through the airport outskirts and then on to a motorway.

"I'll tell you a bit about the school I found for you," Cousin Eunice presently said. "I hope you'll like it. I don't know anybody your age to ask about schools, but I asked the biology professor at my college—his daughter goes to this school—and he recommended it, he said she likes it. Have you really never been to school at all?"

"No, you see we lived too far out. Ma used to get courses and textbooks from some education department and teach us — we even did exams — "

"Well, this is a fairly small school, so I expect you won't find it too hard to get used to it."

"How many?"

"Two hundred."

Two hundred sounded a lot to Cosmo, accustomed to doing lessons with just his brother. He said,

"Where is the school?"

"In Oxford. It's called the Morningquest School, because it was started about a hundred years ago by a Canon Morningquest. It's in a street called the Woodstock Road. The arrangement is that you'll stay as a boarder during the week, and come back to the mill at weekends. That way I can take you in and out by car, because I give lectures in Oxford on Mondays and Fridays. Whereas, if you went in by bus every day, you'd have to get up at five in the morning, and wouldn't be home till nine at night."

"How far is the mill from Oxford, then?"

"About twenty miles. But there isn't a direct bus. Our nearest village is Gitting-under-Edge, and from there you can get a bus to Chipping Norton, and then you have to change buses."

"Couldn't I cycle?"

She cast a quick glance at him and said, "We'll see. Perhaps, in the summer, when you've settled in. But it's a longish way. And I thought, to start with, you'd find it easier to get to know people if you were a boarder. I was always a day-girl when I went to school, and the boarders used to despise the day-people; we always felt inferior and out of everything."

Cosmo didn't voice his views about this. He could see

that Cousin Eunice was trying to do her best for him. He said,

"When do I start there?" not knowing whether school terms in England were the same as those in Australia.

"Next Monday. The term's half through already; you'll only have five weeks of school before the Easter holidays. — I hope you won't be lonely at the mill," she said, sounding doubtful for the first time. "There's absolutely no one living round about. The village is five miles off — it isn't an ideal arrangement."

Here, too, Cosmo kept silent, and refrained from uttering his very different feelings. He would be meeting all those total strangers at school — two hundred of them — the prospect of solitary weekends at the mill was something to hold on to. He asked,

"Isn't there anybody living at Courtoys Place now? I thought that was not far from the mill?"

"It's about three-quarters of a mile away. But you can't talk to the people there."

"Why ever not? Are they mad or something?"

"No, but it's a Ministry of Health research station now. They give people colds and experimental diseases, so they have to stay strictly within bounds and not mix with the general public. They aren't allowed out of the grounds. And all the land round the house — about twenty square miles — is run as an experimental farm. You'll be coming across Mr Marvell, who runs it. He's a nice man. He uses the farm buildings at the Mill House. He has a theory about horses instead of tractors — won't have a tractor on the place. He has Suffolk Punches instead."

"How many?" Cosmo asked with a pricking of interest.

"Five — Queenie, Blossom, Duchess, Prince, and Duke.

– There's Oxford," said Eunice, without any change of tone, nodding sideways to some spires and chimneys, faintly visible through the haze of an early-spring afternoon.

"Shan't we go through it?"

"No, we go round the bypass. It's quicker. You'll soon be seeing plenty of Oxford."

Lob, who had been lying, a huge inert mass in the back of the car, waiting for the journey to pass, evidently began to sniff the air of home and sat up, displacing a strong waft of his strange musty, yeasty smell. Cosmo supposed that Cousin Eunice must have grown accustomed to it by now but, as if drawing the thought out of his mind, she said,

"He does smell ... He's an old, old dog. You can open the window wider if you want. – Now it's only fifteen minutes from here."

They left the motorway at a roundabout and took a smaller road; soon turned off that into one smaller still, and then into a really narrow lane between steep banks that cut off the view; then shortly on to a rutted farm track with gates along it at intervals. The air, when Cosmo got out to open the gates, was moist, fresh and cool; sniffing it, he had a sudden piercingly vivid memory from long, long ago, of wading in a ditch with his brother Mark, the water full and rushing from spring rain – green waterweeds like mermaids' hair swept out in long straight lines – the water going over the tops of his wellingtons ...

"It's grand for me having someone to open the gates," Cousin Eunice said. "Up to now I've had to do it all myself. Lob is no use at all."

"The gates are a nuisance, aren't they?"

"Yes, but they keep out trespassers and picnickers. Mr Marvell's very particular about gates being always kept shut, otherwise people leave smashed beer-bottles in his fields, and the Jerseys eat bits of glass and die a horrible death."

She nodded sideways again at some small elegant mouse-coloured cows with huge black-ringed eyes. "That's why there are such fierce signs on the gates."

The signs said, "Department of the Environment Experimental Farm Strictly NO admission except on Official Business".

"That's the last gate," Cousin Eunice said as Cosmo clanged it shut. "Now we're nearly home."

The track ran here, unfenced, between two prune-coloured fields of ploughed earth with faint green shoots in straight lines; then they skirted round a long high furry ridge of leafless trees, and Cousin Eunice put the Rolls into low gear.

"It gets quite steep here, and there are badgers some-times."

The track dropped downhill between high banks — a tunnel, with trees meeting overhead; then they came out into a circle of green meadow with the steep wooded hillside curving round it in a horseshoe.

"Oh, I remember *this*," said Cosmo.

"How old were you when you came here? Six? Well, it's not a place to forget."

Ahead of them stood the house: old red-brown brick, partly timbered, black beams crossing it in a zigzag pattern, the roof gold with lichen, and big trees close by. Then the river, looping round, meeting the wood on either side, making an almost-island of the great meadow; and beyond the house a wooden footbridge leading to a real island, and the mill buildings.

"Can you swim?" said Cousin Eunice in sudden doubt.

"You've been in the middle of Australia for so long – how many years?"

"Five. Nearly six. But we used to go for holidays to a place called Coff's Harbour. I can swim quite well," Cosmo assured her.

"That's a relief. Just the same you want to watch it by the weir. There's a terrific undertow – you'd be scraped along the bottom for a hundred yards if you fell in there. So be careful, won't you. The river's okay – the Dribble, your father and I used to call it. – There's Mrs Tydings."

Cosmo had another sudden rush of memory at the sight of the figure – like a stocky, active shrew-mouse in a blue-and-white print apron, with black strap shoes and bobbed white hair kept fiercely back by one grip – who shot out of the door as the car slowed to a halt. Lob was already standing up, impatient to have the door opened.

"Well, Miss Eunice, you found him all right then, I see. Made good time home, you did. Tea's all ready. And after he's had his tea, I expect *he'd* better go straight to bed. Thirty hours in the air – dear, dear! Well, you *have* shot up and no mistake," she said, surveying Cosmo. "I daresay it's all them eucalyptus trees – they say it makes the climate healthy. I don't suppose you remember me, do you?"

"Yes I do," said Cosmo. "You gave me a duck's egg, and lived in a little house across the lawn, and kept chickens, and had a cat called Bubbles, a grey cat."

"Well I never! I've still got her – she's twelve now. Fancy you remembering. Come along now – I just put the tea to mash. – And how's your father keeping?"

Cosmo made most noncommittal reply as he followed her indoors, carrying some of the luggage. The first room was huge – he found he remembered that too – brick floor, stairs leading up, a big hearth where a wood fire burned, a comfortable sagging sofa and armchairs, a refectory table strewn with papers and books. And a smaller table near the fireplace, set for tea.

After tea — potato-scones, blackberry jelly, and nut-cake — Cosmo did begin to feel as if he could sleep for a hundred years. But he said,

"Can I go out and have a look round? Just for a little?"

"Don't get lost now, or fall in the weir!" snapped Mrs Tydings, but Cousin Eunice said easily,

"He'll be all right, Emma; a bit of fresh air will help him get off to sleep. Go ahead, Cosmo; you'll have to come in soon when it gets dark anyway."

The air outside smelt mysterious — of water, and twilight, and growing things. A path of huge stone flags led across the velvet square of mossy grass in the angle of the L-shaped house — and he had another memory: trying, at six years old, to jump from one to the next, and not quite being able to. Mark, four years older, could do it easily ...

He went to the footbridge first and stood on it for a long time, looking down into the clear water beneath, pouring, plaiting, racing past; it made very little noise, it was in such a hurry to reach the end of the island. But on the other side, past the mill buildings — he would not go into them tonight, they looked too dark and spooky, and Cousin Eunice had warned him that the floors were rotten and treacherous, and the machinery likely to fall through at any moment — on the other side of the island, there was the weir, tons of water hurling down in a smother of foam. The noise on this side was tremendous — funny that by the bridge it was so quiet. Indeed, when he had re-crossed the island, and stood on the bridge again, he quite clearly heard a voice that seemed to be addressing him. It said, in a mild, conversational tone,

"Oh, you're back then. Where's the other boy? Weren't there two of you?"

Surprised, he looked round; he had thought he was alone. He could see nobody, but the voice had seemed to come from the track that followed the river-bank to the corner of the meadow where the wood sloped up – opposite to the way they had come in the car. It was there, he remembered, that the brook came hopping down in a series of waterfalls – the brook he and Mark had dammed. And there had been a third boy helping them – what was his name? The voice had brought his memory back.

But although Cosmo followed the track right into the wood and up the steep ascent, he saw no one. Whoever had spoken to him must have slipped away very quickly and quietly. He found the brook, though, smaller than he had remembered, and rather choked up with dead brushwood and leaves. I'll clear it out tomorrow, he thought. Perhaps then whoever it was will come back.

Up in the field above the wood he heard a sudden tremendous thunder of huge hoofs, and remembered Mr Marvell and his five Suffolk Punches, Prince, Blossom, Queenie, Duchess, and Duke. One of them must be up there kicking his heels in a last massive caper before dark fell. They would be something to see tomorrow too …

From the house he heard Cousin Eunice's shout.

"Cosmo! Cooee! Time for bed."

His room was the same one that he had shared with Mark: long and cornery, with a wardrobe covering the whole of one end, a very low windowsill, and a sloping ceiling. A bookshelf held old books with gilt-edged pages that had belonged to Cosmo's father.

"Here's a torch for the night," Cousin Eunice said. "Don't forget where the bathroom is – down three steps and on the left. That's new since you were here last. And my room is opposite, in case you need anything, or can't sleep."

"Where's Mrs Tydings?"

"Oh, she's still in her own cottage, across the lawn."

"Cousin Eunice," he said, "do you remember a boy who used to come and play with Mark and me when we were here before? His name was Len or Ken or Tom – something like that?"

But Cousin Eunice – who had not, after all, been at home during that visit – could not remember any such boy.

Stretched in his comfortably sagging bed, feeling like a wrung-out rag, Cosmo took his diary – a small, thick book – from his jacket pocket, and wrote: "Came to Courtoys Mill. Cousin Eunice seems okay. The island ... "

Then the pen rolled from his fingers and he slept.

2

Elder Brothers

A SLAPPING, GUSTY RAIN WAS falling on Monday as Cousin Eunice drove Cosmo in to Oxford. He was wearing for the first time the Morningquest school uniform which had been ordered beforehand for him (his father had sent the measurements from Australia). The uniform was severe – black raincoat and blazer, white shirt, grey trousers, and a grey, black and white striped tie.

"You look like a stockbroker," Cousin Eunice said.

But she herself looked unexpectedly businesslike and formidable too, in a tailored suit and nylons and her yellow hair done up very tight, instead of the jeans, sweater, and loose plait she had worn over the weekend. In the back of the car she had chucked a voluminous black gown, to be worn when she gave her lectures, she said. "It frightens the students and makes them pay attention because I look like Dracula's aunt." What was the lecture about, Cosmo wanted to know.

"It's about solving equations of the fifth degree, which are supposed to be insoluble."

"*Are* they? Why?"

"Lots of things are still insoluble," Cousin Eunice said.

"Even though solutions may exist, we can't get at them. Or explain happenings, even though we can see them happening. I was reading, the other day, about a boy who makes sculptures out of paperclips, without touching them. He can do it even if the paperclips are sealed up inside a glass globe."

"How?"

"It isn't known how. But he does it. And not by magic. Or rather, it's what would have been called magic two hundred years ago – he'd probably have been burned as a witch. Now we know it's something to do with radiation, with vibrations; people have moved bits of metal through walls in the same way, without making a hole in the wall, without bending the metal. What it amounts to is that we have got a wrong idea about matter. Some things can be in two places at once."

Cosmo felt that he was losing his grasp, but he hung on grimly.

"Perhaps it's our idea of *time* that's wrong? *At once* – when you say two places at once – maybe that's not what we think? When I was coming here from Australia, time kept sliding about; the plane got to some places before it had started. And if we were on a distant star looking at the earth, we'd still be seeing things that happened long ago."

"Yes; something like that." A great slap of rain poured over the windscreen, and she doubled the speed of the wipers. "I do hope you have a good science teacher at the Morningquest; Dick Soames said he thinks the man isn't too bad. He's called Mr Ramsden."

"I *wish* I didn't have to go to school," Cosmo said. "I'm sure school was invented just because parents can't be bothered to look after their children."

Cousin Eunice considered this.

"Very possibly. But there are some advantages to it. After all, specially nowadays, you do have to learn a lot of things, just to keep alive; look how useless babies are, they don't even know how to prise the lids off treacle tins. They wouldn't last a day without help. What schools *ought* to be—I don't say they are—is places where you can pick up all that kind of know-how very quickly and compactly. And, of course, make friends, learn how to get on with other people."

Cosmo felt he could have done without that part.

Cousin Eunice said,

"I haven't talked to you about your mother and Mark."

He had been grateful for this.

"I thought you'd probably rather not, just yet," she went on. "But, if you want to, at any time—sometimes it does help to talk—"

Just at that moment he could not have talked. His throat was stuck. He could not even nod. Seeing this, she went on, changing the subject, "Now you must be sure and let me know if there's anything at school that you need and haven't got. I went all through that fearsome printed list, but lists don't always cover everything. Mrs Robinson (she's the matron) said it would be all right for me to phone you this evening at about five. And then if you find you need a—a briefcase, or a magnet, or something I haven't thought of—I could get it for you and drop it at the school during the course of the week."

"But I thought you didn't come in to Oxford again till Friday?"

"Oh," she said, "sometimes I come in to go shopping. Old Lob likes a shopping trip now and then—he enjoys the town smells. And so does Emma."

Lob had elected to stay at home today after one look at the weather, settling down with a sigh on the big hearthstone that still held the warmth of yesterday's blazing fire.

It had been a good weekend, on the whole. Cosmo had discovered, on Saturday, that he did not, after all, want to dam the brook again, or not just yet; it made him remember Mark too vividly. Instead he climbed up through the wood and made friends with Mr Marvell and Prince and Blossom, who were pulling a plough through black, sticky, chocolate-cake earth, and then with Duke and Duchess, who were drawing a tumbril with mangolds for the sheep; he had been allowed to ride on Duchess's broad back. And then he had explored the island, which was all grown over with elder-bushes and was going to be very nettly soon; it would make a grand place for a fort. On Sunday he had helped Cousin Eunice prune trees in the orchard and clip a yew-hedge with very efficient electric clippers. In the afternoon it had rained, but then there was the great fire in the stone hearth, and all father's books.

His own were following by boat.

"When you start making friends at school, you can bring people back for weekends," Cousin Eunice said. "There are lots of bedrooms."

"Oh, I don't suppose I'll want to do that."

"Here we are," she said.

They had been driving down the Woodstock Road for what seemed an endless time; it was a wide road with large middle-aged houses on each side, set back behind low walls and shiny laurelly evergreen trees; some of the gardens had crocuses in them and a few daffodils. Now the Rolls drew to a stately halt in the semicircular drive of a particularly large, high house with a front all decorated with pinnacles and stone balconies; there were two huge stone balls ornamenting the balustrade on each side of the three front steps.

"The Rolls ought to get you off to a good start, anyway," Cousin Eunice said.

An old man (Goodger, the odd-job man, Cosmo later learned) came and took his luggage out of the boot, giving the car a respectful and affectionate look as he did so. Boys and girls of varying ages were pouring in through front and side gates; the boys wore the same uniform as Cosmo, the girls, under their black raincoats, had grey skirts and long black socks.

A grey-haired woman ("Mrs Robinson, the matron," hissed Cousin Eunice) was in the front hall to meet them. She had kind dark eyes and skin like uncooked pastry, pale and a little soggy; she wore a twin-set and a houndstooth check skirt. "So this is Cosmo," she said in a gentle Scottish voice. "Well, and we're very glad to have you with us, Cosmo, even so late in the term. Now I'm sure you have lots of things to do, Professor Doom, so I'll not be keeping you."

"That means she wants to get rid of me," said Cousin Eunice to Cosmo. "So I'll say goodbye for now, and see you on Friday about four o'clock. And I'll phone you this evening at five." She ran down the front steps with a quick flip of her hand.

"A very distinguished lady, Professor Doom," Mrs Robinson said. "That's right, Goodger, take Cosmo's cases up to Ruskin dormitory. You are lucky to have an aunt like that, I daresay she'll be no end of help to you with your maths and science. Now I'll just show you where your bedroom is, and then it will be time for prayers. And after that I know Mr Gabbitas wants a word with you; he's the headmaster, as you probably know."

Cosmo followed Mrs Robinson, deciding not to correct the mistake about Eunice being his aunt; what did it matter, anyway? The stairs were covered with tremendously thick, durable coconut matting, and there were old school photographs, with dates, all the way up the wall. Above, a strong smell of lino and furniture polish, and doors opening on to classrooms; then up again, more stairs, to a higher landing, where there were dormitories, containing, he was glad to see, only four or five beds each; he had imagined long rows like hospital wards.

"Here is yours, Ruskin, and this is your bed in the corner," Mrs Robinson said. Goodger had already left his cases. There was a chest-of-drawers, a chair, and a wash-stand. "You can unpack tonight, there won't be time now. I'll take you down to your form-room, you are in Remove."

"What is Remove?"

"It is the name of the form that you are in," Mrs Robinson said patiently. "There are the Juniors at the bottom of the school, then first, second, and third Preparatories, then Remove, that's you, then first and second Intermediate, then first, second, and third Shell, and then the Seniors. So you are about in the middle."

"What queer names."

"Shell comes from the French *échelle*, that means a ladder. Now, here is your form-room."

They were down on the floor below again. Mrs Robinson opened a door to display a room full of busily occupied grey-and-white figures who were getting books out of lockers and putting them on tables.

"Charley!" she called. "This is Cosmo Curtoys, will you show him where he's to sit and take him over to prayers. And why is your tie such a mess, may I ask?" She untied, retied, and tightened the offending tie in three swift movements. Charley, a boy who was freckled all over like a bird's egg, submitted with a resigned grin.

"Right, then, Cosmo, I'll be seeing ye later." Mrs Robinson vanished as a bell began to ring.

"That's for prayers," said Charley. "Come on."

Everybody in the room – there seemed about a dozen, in fact there were ten as Cosmo later discovered – clattered down the stairs, out through a side-door, down some iron steps, and along a covered way to the school hall, which was a large wooden building with a stage at one end. Cosmo noticed on the way a wintry-looking garden, a hard tennis-court which was at present one huge puddle with yellow leaves floating in it, a swing, a see-saw, a stretch of soggy lawn, some gravel paths. It all looked dismal.

In the school hall they stood in rows, a row to a form. Cosmo, squinting sideways, found that there were four girls and six boys in his row, not counting himself. Several people turned and stared at him from rows in front; he felt very conspicuous in his new, tidy uniform.

Two people, a man and a woman, came briskly on to the platform; a hymn was sung – "He who would valiant be" – one that Cosmo knew, which was a relief – prayers were said, then they all dispersed again. The members of Remove went back to their classroom, where they found a red-nosed, sandy-haired man waiting for them.

"Ah, we have a new member today, Cosmo Curtoys," he said. "You had better sit there, Cosmo."

There were three tables in the room, with four chairs at each; the man indicated an empty place, and Cosmo went to it and sat down. He was beside a girl with plaits, who gave him a cool look.

"Actually you pronounce my name Curtis," he said to the sandy man.

"I beg your pardon?"

"My name. It's pronounced Curtis."

A titter ran round the room. Cosmo flushed.

"You should always put up your hand before speaking to a member of the staff," the sandy man told him. "Right: Curtis it shall be. I hope you have all imbibed *that* piece of information," he said to the rest of the form. "Cosmo has just come from Australia; I daresay he will be able to tell us all about marsupials and, er, *billabongs*, when it comes to geography. At present, however, we have to address ourselves to the decimal system."

Cosmo had done the decimal system and found it no problem. But after about ten minutes a head poked round the door and said,

"Cosmo Curtoys to the headmaster's office."

"He prefers his name to be pronounced *Curtis*," said the sandy-haired man. Everybody laughed openly this time. Cosmo stood up with hot cheeks. What was so funny about his name, for heaven's sake?

He followed the head (it belonged to one of the boys from the Senior form) along a highly-polished passage to a half-open door.

"Here's Cosmo Curtoys, sir." He made no attempt to pronounce the name correctly, perhaps feeling that Cosmo was too young for such a privilege.

"Ah yes; come in, and shut the door."

Mr Gabbitas, the headmaster, was the white-haired man who had read the prayers. He had a face, Cosmo thought, like a Saluki, long, and rather sweet; he should have long drooping silky ears on either side to complete the effect.

"Sit down, my dear Curtis," (*he* got the name right.) "I won't keep you a minute, because I expect you will be wanting to get to know your form-mates." Cosmo did not argue about this but sat down as directed. The headmaster's room was small and snug with three very interesting pictures on the walls; he would have liked to take a good look at them, but Mr Gabbitas was saying,

"Now, all this will seem quite strange to you for a while, I expect; your cousin tells me that you were living right out in the wilds and having lessons sent by post, is that right? Seeing such a lot of strange faces will be rather tiring for you at first, but I expect you will soon settle down; this is not *really* such a big school, and I hope that you will find us all a very friendly set of people."

He paused and smiled and Cosmo felt he was expected to say something but could not think of anything suitable.

"Now," went on Mr Gabbitas, "I have decided – I have talked about this with the other members of the staff here and *we* have decided – that, on the whole, it will be more sensible if we don't tell the other boys and girls in the school about your sad *loss*."

Loss, thought Cosmo stolidly; he picked the right word there.

"You have been through a very unhappy time," Mr Gabbitas continued, "and we think it will be best for you if it is not talked about and discussed and made into a *mystery*; which can so easily happen, can't it?"

"Yes, sir."

"So all that has been said about you, Cosmo, is that your relatives are in Australia, and you have come over here by yourself to go to school, and are staying with your very distinguished cousin. And, if you agree, we'll keep it that way."

"Yes, sir."

"Are you quite happy about this, eh? You agree that it's best to put painful things behind you – just try and take part in the ordinary life of the school. Where I am sure you will soon find friends."

"Yes, sir."

"However," Mr Gabbitas went on, "I don't know if your cousin has told you that, as well as being a headmaster, I am a psychiatrist; that is, a kind of mind-doctor. If you find at any time, Cosmo, that you feel unhappy or worried or *puzzled* – that you aren't managing to settle down – you can always come and see me and I'll try to help you. Just tell your form-master, Mr Cheevy – or Mrs Robinson – and they will fix a time for you to come. All right? Now you had better run along, as we are both going to be very busy." He gave Cosmo a sweet – rather too sweet? – smile, creasing up his eyes, to show that the interview was over, and Cosmo found his way back to the Remove form-room. Well, anyway, he thought, now I know that the sandy-haired man is called Mr Cheevy.

During the day he got the rest of his form sorted out. The four girls were Rebecca, Sheil, Tansy and Meredith. Rebecca was German, large, fair-haired, and cheerfully good at everything she did. Sheil was small and silent, with a slight cast in one eye; Tansy had bright brown ringlets and giggled a lot; Meredith was the dark girl with plaits who had given him the cool measuring look when he first sat down.

The boys were not so easy to sort out because there were more of them. Cosmo could see at once that the freckled Charley was the form leader; he was so, not because he was brighter than the rest, but because he was so tremendously active and confident; and his friend Molesworth, whom everyone called Moley, was therefore the second-in-command, not because of any commanding qualities, but because he was Charley's friend. Moley, actually, seemed quite decent; he was rather quiet and pale, with an unimpressive face, but he had a habit of making short, dry, funny remarks. Often these were in such a low voice that only the people sitting at his own table caught them, but Cosmo heard one; as Mr Cheevy gathered up his books and left the room when the bell went at the end of the period, Cosmo noticed that the master's hands shook quite badly; a couple of papers slipped from his grasp and the obliging Rebecca leapt to pick them up and hand them back.

"*He* won't win the egg-and-spoon race," muttered Moley, deadpan.

Cosmo was surprised into laughing, and several people looked at him with raised eyebrows; evidently newcomers were not supposed to laugh at jokes.

It was easy to pick out the form outcast; that was the boy called Tom Bunthorne, whom everybody, including the staff, addressed as Bun. He was a big, heavy boy, clumsy in his movements and always in a muddle; he was never able to answer a single question correctly, and the remarks he made were so stupid that everybody sighed when he opened his mouth. But he never gave up trying; he had a big, hopeful smile that showed a lot of unbrushed teeth. His skin was dry and flaky and he smelt rather badly too—a sweetish musty smell, not unlike that of Lob, thought Cosmo, who was sitting between him and Meredith. Evidently before Cosmo's arrival Bun had been stuck by himself at the end of a table.

Then there were a couple of boys who were friends, and talked almost exclusively to each other: Andy and Lot, they were called, Cosmo discovered later; they were dayboys and disappeared at lunchtime, going off to Lot's house where they both had lunch; Cosmo began to see what

34

Cousin Eunice had meant about day-boys being left out of things.

Lunch was something of a trial. The dining-room was huge, with ten tables that each held twenty people; everybody raced in when the gong went, and friends kept places for each other, sometimes bagging whole sides of tables for groups or gangs.

"You want to sit by me?" Bun offered with his hopeful smile.

"All right," Cosmo said resignedly. There was only one place left, so he had to; but he could see already that to be Bun's friend was to share his isolation; it was like touching a leper and catching his disease. Probably Bun tried to make friends with every new boy who came, and as soon as they found anybody better they dropped him. His rough-skinned face, with its pale eyes and ever-open mouth seemed to hold already the expectation of this disappointment.

Mrs Robinson, on Cosmo's other side, was at the end of the table, serving slices of cold meat.

"Cosmo's from Australia," she told the table at large. "He'll be able to tell us all about the bush. Have you seen lots of kangaroos, Cosmo?"

Cosmo felt himself redden as everybody looked at him. It seemed so dull to confess that he had lived in a part where there were no kangaroos. He said,

"Well, I did see one once, when my mother and I were crossing the desert in a Landrover. We stopped at night to sleep, and I woke up and went for a walk. It was moonlight and I saw what I thought was a funny-shaped tree-stump, so I walked towards it, and it got up and hopped away."

Quite a few people laughed, but he noticed disbelieving expressions on the faces of Charley and Moley, who were

35

sitting at the top of the table. And of course they were right; the episode was a true one, but it had happened to his brother Mark, not to him. He had been too small for that trip, but Mark had told him about it.

He was thankful when most people at the table began talking about some football match and forgot him; except Bun, that is, who plied him with boring questions about Australia until the end of the meal.

In the afternoon people were supposed to play football or hockey, but as the rain was still pelting down there were indoor sports in the school hall, taken by Mr Breadbury, the games master, an irascible little man with bright red spots on each cheekbone, who was frightfully quick at giving orders in a shrill shout.

"Now we'll play Do This and Do That— *do this!*" He stood on one leg. "*Do that!*" He bent down and put his head between his legs. "Do this!" He sank down like a frog. "You — new boy— you're out!" Cosmo, who had never heard of the game, gathered confusedly that you were supposed to obey one set of orders but not the other. Everybody looked at him despisingly.

Then they played hideous games with bags of beans, tossing them from hand to hand at top speed, one team trying to race the other. Cosmo was hopeless at those too, but a lot of the other boys were equally bad; only the girls shone here, whipping the bags nimbly from one to the next. Then they played an even worse game, where one team stood in the circle made by the other team and had a football hurled at their legs; you were supposed to jump into the air to avoid the ball. When it hit you, you were out. Here Charley, bouncing, agile, and seemingly tireless, stayed in longer than anybody except the German Rebecca. Charley's friend Moley did not take part in these games; he had a weak heart, somebody said; he sat cross-legged against the wall, shouting encouragement to his friend.

Cosmo was immensely relieved when this period was over and they went on to a physics lesson with the red-headed Mr Ramsden; it was good to be in a real lab with benches and retorts and bunsen-burners, things that Mark and he had always longed for as they tried to do experiments out of *The Boy's Book of Practical Science*.

Then there was tea: bread and jam and strong tea like tar-water. Instead of the staff, as at lunch, members of the Senior form sat at the heads of tables and poured the tea. Bun again hopefully kept a place for Cosmo, and Cosmo again resignedly sat in it.

Then there were two hours of homework, done in silence. During this period Eunice phoned. No, Cosmo told her, he was fine; he needed nothing. Yes, school was okay; no, truly, he didn't want anything. Which was true, except, perhaps, to fall down a black well for ever. "See you on Friday, then," she said, and hung up.

Then there was supper, sardines on toast and stewed apple. By now the day seemed to have been going on for about six months.

As they left the dining-room he happened to be beside Meredith, and he asked her,

"What do we do *now*?"

"Whatever you like," she said coolly. "You are free till bedtime, which is half-past eight for our lot."

"What are you going to do?"

"Piano practice," she said, and took a music case from a rack, and walked away.

Cosmo went back to his form-room. Charley, Moley, Rebecca, Sheil, Tansy and another boy were there; instantly, on entering the room, Cosmo had the uncomfortable

37

feeling that they had been talking about him. He went to his locker and pretended to hunt among the books that had been given him.

"Who do you hate worst in the school, Rebecca?" said Tansy, breaking the silence with her giggle.

"Miss Mossop. Ugh! She's like a rotten potato."

"Chris?"

"Bun. Wish he'd catch Housemaid's Knee and Athlete's Foot and Tennis Elbow and die."

They all laughed.

"Charley? Who do you hate worst?"

Charley pondered. "Old Gabby Gabbitas," he said at last. "Because of his do-gooding."

"Moley?"

"Oh, I dunno. Yes I do. The picture of our Sainted Foun-dah, dear old Canon Morningquest, over the middle dining table. It makes me want to re-gurgi-tate."

They laughed again.

Cosmo, pretending that he had found what he came for, retreated. He could hear a buzz of talk break out as soon as he closed the door.

Wandering without purpose he remembered that, in the basement, next to the lab where they had done their physics, another door had a sign that said PLAYROOM.

He made his way to it, along a damp basement passage that smelt of laundry and shoe-polish. There were voices coming from inside this door also, and he opened it with wary apprehension, as one might approach cannibals dancing round a boiling pot. But inside the room, which was large and cold and contained a pingpong table and a Corinthian bagatelle board, there were only two people. He recognized them as members of the form below Remove who had joined in the sports that afternoon: a boy and girl

38

called Frances and Tim. They had pushed the pingpong table against the wall and were sliding on the polished lino, trying to achieve one complete turn as they slid the length of the room.

Cosmo watched them for a while.

"D'you want to play pingpong?" asked the girl Frances, who looked quite good-natured.

"No thanks," he said quickly, and then wished he had said Yes. Mark and he had played a lot, and Ma sometimes joined in; she was formidably good. He wandered aimlessly back upstairs and found with relief that it was nearly half-past eight and he could go to bed. The other three boys with whom he shared Ruskin dormitory were all from different forms, and older; they went to bed later. He was able to get undressed and into bed before they appeared, but he could not sleep; his heart felt as heavy as if a magnet were dragging it down. However he pretended to be asleep when the elders came up, so as not to have to talk to them. One of them said,

"He comes from Australia, doesn't he?" evidently with a nod towards Cosmo.

"Umn. Was telling some story about bumping into a kangaroo in the dark. Didn't sound true."

"Wonder why he comes *now*, in the middle of term," somebody yawned.

"I bags the first bath."

"Don't be too long then, you stinker."

At last the lights were out. And at last, clutching under his pillow the diary, in which he had written, "First day at school. Vile place", Cosmo went to sleep. As soon as he slept, he began to dream about the brook at Courtoys Mill. He and Mark were wading up it, searching, searching, and calling, calling, for the boy called Len or Ken. And the

39

water was coming in over the tops of his boots.

By the end of the week Cosmo had a kind of skeleton idea of school life. He knew, for instance, that Mademoiselle, who taught French, was not taken seriously; nor was Miss Gracie, who taught singing; in fact everybody gave her a hellish time. On the other hand Mr Kelly, who taught Latin, was received with the deepest silence and respect, because he had a waspish habit of pulling people's hair if he considered they were being impertinent or inattentive. Mrs Robinson was kind and sensible; so was Miss Nivven, who taught English, and who had told Cosmo about the library, which was a useful refuge after supper; though he had now fallen into the habit of sliding with Tim and Frances for a while every evening. It was dull, but better than staying in his own form-room, where he felt under constant silent criticism. If Charley did not like you, then nobody could display too much friendship, and Charley was in no hurry to be welcoming. Nor was Mr Cheevy, the form-master, who tended to scowl when his bloodshot eye fell on Cosmo. One day, arriving early and finding Cosmo the only one there, getting out his maths books, he said abruptly,

"Your father was Richard Curtoys, wasn't he?" – giving the name its correct pronunciation.

"Yes. He's still alive," Cosmo said.

"You should call me sir."

"Sir."

"Why did he leave England? He was doing useful work in cancer research. Why did he choose to give it all up and go and bury himself in the bush?"

"I don't know," Cosmo said. "Sir."

For the first time he consciously wondered why the family *had* moved to Australia. He had been only six at the

40

time and had accepted the move matter-of-factly. Before that they had lived in London. He could dimly remember a house in Hampstead, sailing boats on the ponds. He might ask Cousin Eunice about it.

"Perhaps he thought it would be healthier," he said. "Sir."

"That sounds to me like rubbish."

Mr Cheevy seemed personally annoyed about it; his watery eyes glared, his damp skin sweated with irritation.

"What was he doing out there, anyway? In the bush?"

"Practising as a doctor. Only there weren't many patients. He used to have to drive hundreds of miles, sometimes, to get to sick people. And he wrote articles for magazines. And I think a book, too. – Anyway, he's going to come back," Cosmo added.

"*Oh?* He is, is he? And do what?"

"I don't know. Something here, in Oxford," Cosmo said. "Sir."

Then the rest of the form came into the room, and Mr Cheevy stopped catechizing Cosmo. But after that he was just a little more friendly in his tone.

"Well, how did it go?" Cousin Eunice said in the Rolls on Friday.

Cosmo could hardly put into words that she seemed what a hovering helicopter might to a shipwrecked mariner on a desert island. Even the smell of Lob, sitting up to give Cosmo a dignified welcome in the back of the car, was homely and comforting, compared with that of blackboard chalk and furniture polish.

"Oh," he said. "All right, I suppose."

She glanced at him sideways.

"Cheer up! It really does take a while to get used to.

Anyway, it's going to be a fine weekend, and Mrs Tydings has got a chicken for supper."

"Cousin Eunice," he said. "Why did Father decide to move to Australia?"

"Oh," she said thoughtfully. "I wondered if you'd ask me that."

"Is it so important?"

"Dick never talked to you about it? After – after they went?"

"No, never."

She reflected for a while, and then said, "Well, Dick told me to use my discretion about what I told you. I personally think *everyone* should be told *everything*. Because, for a start, you can't keep things from people for ever – something always leaks out sooner or later – and then you're in worse trouble. People are sore at not being told in the first place; and bad news always gets worse with keeping."

All this made Cosmo anxious. He wondered what it was leading up to. Something horrible?

"Is it to do with Mother and Mark too?"

"Yes," she said, "it is. But, look, here we are nearly home, and I want to sow some runner-beans before supper. I'll tell you this evening after supper, okay?"

"Okay, Cousin Eunice," he said, getting out to open the gate.

"You can call me Eunice if you want," she shouted through the driver's window. "Cousin is such a mouthful."

Already, coming back to the mill house seemed like returning home. The trees had rather more leaves than they had last week, and he remembered the quadruple notes of a blackbird's shout, in the lilac by the flagged path.

Mrs Tydings was there to greet them.

"Now you get those school clothes off, Cosmo, directly,

or I know how it'll be, you'll be over on the island or up in the woods and they'll be covered with mud and filth. I've your jeans washed and ironed and all your sweaters darned ... "

Up in his bedroom he found that, during the week, Cousin Eunice had had a desk built for him along the window-wall, with drawers and cupboards underneath, and a table-lamp, so that he could do his homework there. He had quite a lot of it, as a matter of fact: maths, geography, and an essay about Roman Britain. He decided to do it all first thing tomorrow morning and get it out of the way. But in the meantime he was going out: he had an idea for building a tree-house in the huge old walnut tree that grew in the lawn to the side of the house.

He went out and inspected it thoughtfully. The trunk was massive, as big as an elm or chestnut, and the first branches didn't start till seventeen or eighteen feet up. What he would need was either a rope ladder or some of those things like big steel staples that linesmen stick in the sides of telegraph poles to climb up them. He wondered where he could get those. Mr Marvell would know. Then there was a big flattish fork where three, four, five branches stuck out in different directions; he would need some planks to fit across there; a hammer, nails ...

"Have you got a fairly high ladder?" he asked Eunice, over the chicken.

"There's an apple-picking ladder in the barn – would that do?"

"Don't you go breaking your neck, now," warned Mrs Tydings. "Boys – dear, dear! Once you have one in the house, there's never an easy moment."

After the chicken there was a very good blackcurrant pudding (their own currants, bottled from last year, Mrs

43

Tydings said) but by now Cosmo's stomach felt nervous, he could only eat a small helping.

"Were there Romans in these parts, Cousin Eunice?" he asked, trying to distract himself, thinking of his homework.

"Certainly there were; right here, as a matter of fact. We had archaeologists one summer digging about in the garden and the field. There was a dye factory here."

"A *dye factory*?" He thought of factory chimneys and noisy machinery. "Doesn't sound like Romans."

"No, they would have had big vats of dyes and people chopping up woad and madder, making them into powders to dye blue and red, and burning sulphur to bleach cloth white. No pollution laws in those days. All the land round about was probably forest then." She sighed. "Finished? Let's sit by the fire. We'll wash up later."

Mrs Tydings came and sat with them, vigorously knitting something from thick blue wool, scowling over it in concentration, pursing and unpursing her lips.

Cousin Eunice said,

"You know our family is very old – it goes a tremendously long way back. Well, of course, everybody's family is old, obviously we're all descended from *somebody* – but *we* happen to know a good deal about our ancestors."

"Why is that?"

"Well there was an abbey at Dorchester, you know, where the monks used to keep chronicles – records; monasteries were a bit like public libraries in the middle ages, they were where all the documents and information tended to be kept, because the monks knew how to read and write when most people didn't. And monasteries were a bit safer from attack than other places. Records were kept in Dorchester Abbey from the seventh century on – maybe earlier – because the Bishops of Mercia had their headquarters there—Mercia was the largest diocese in England. Dorchester is a much older town than Oxford. And anyway, in the monks' chronicles at Dorchester Abbey there was this record of the Curtoys family. You've certainly got both Roman and British ancestry—the name probably comes from the Latin *curtus*, meaning short—although later, when the Normans got involved, it was thought that it might derive from old French words, *corteis* or *cortois*, meaning polite, courtly, educated. So you can take your choice about that."

"What about the Dooms?"

"Oh, the Dooms came over with the Danes; Doom really means judgment, and a Doomsman was a kind of judge; there have always been a lot of lawyers in the Doom family, like my father. And a lot of intermarriages between Dooms and Curtoyses from way back."

"So what has all this got to do with Father deciding to go to Australia?"

"I'm coming to that. It was your mother really," said Cousin Eunice. "You see—it just sounds too fanciful for words, but there's no way of putting it except the flat truth —there's a hereditary curse on the Curtoys family. I daresay if you hadn't been in Australia, you would have been bound to find out about it sooner. I don't see how Dick could have gone on keeping it dark—"

"A *curse*? You're *kidding*?"

"No, a bona fide curse."

Mrs Tydings sighed, jabbed her needles into her knitting, and started winding a new ball of wool off the skein. Cousin Eunice dropped another log on the fire, which sputtered and crackled and sent out a puff of aromatic blue smoke.

"There was an ancient British temple in the woods

45

somewhere round here," Eunice went on, "and the Romans came bustling along, tidying things up the way the Romans tended to do, and closed it down, said it would be better if the people worshipped Mithras or Jupiter instead of their forest gods. Well, I daresay they didn't mean to be rough about it, but there was a boy working in the temple then, a kind of acolyte or altar-boy, I suppose, and he went bolting out and defied the Romans, and there was a bit of a scuffle, and one of the Roman soldiers ran the boy through with his sword. Killed him – very likely he didn't mean to. The boy was the son of the priestess, so then *she* went and stabbed herself, on the altar. And that left only the old, old priestess, who was the boy's grandmother, and she put a curse on the Roman soldier."

"What was the curse?" Cosmo was immensely interested in the story, though he found it hard to believe in the curse. He imagined the temple – a big wooden building, with pillars, maybe, and smoke coiling between them from the sacred fires, rather dim inside, and the priestess in a blue robe, looking like Cousin Eunice, and the old, old priestess like Mrs Tydings. And what would the boy look like?

"Oh, the priestess said, 'I curse you by Toutatus, the god of war, and Vaun, the god of the forest. May your firstborn son die in battle at an early age, and may his mother die of grief at his loss, and may this go on from generation to generation.' That was the gist of it."

"And did that happen?"

"Well, we don't know so much about the early ancestors, the Romans and Saxons. People generally *did* die at an early age in those days, whether in battle or just because life was tough. But it's certainly quite noticeable later. There was a fourteen-year-old Curtoys who died at the battle of Crécy, and his mother fell down dead of heart-failure when she heard the news. Eustace Curtoys died at Agincourt – he was fifteen; his mother died of grief. Thomas Curtoys died at Bosworth – he was on King Richard's side – he was sixteen; his mother died a month later. Oh, and there was one at Blenheim and one at Salamanca and one on the north-west frontier – and your uncle Frank in the Battle of Britain – "

"I never even knew I *had* an uncle Frank," Cosmo said. He had begun to shiver.

"Well, you didn't. He died before you were born. Your father had a miserable childhood because *his* mother died when he was ten. He had been eight years younger than his brother Frank – "

"The *younger* brothers are all right – they don't die?" Now Cosmo was shivering even more. He reached over and poked the fire, as an excuse to get closer to the warmth.

A bright flame broke out, illuminating Eunice's face. She looked sad, but resolute, as if she were lancing a boil on someone's foot.

"The younger brothers don't die. They carry on the line. But their eldest sons die."

"So that was why Mother and M-M-Mark – "

"Your father hadn't told your mother about this. Not at first, I mean. He said it was all a pack of rubbish, he wouldn't believe it. He *shut his eyes to it*," Eunice said angrily and violently. "So she married him, not knowing – "

"He shouldn't have done that."

Cosmo loved his father – who was clever, funny, sympathetic, tremendously learned, knew about all kinds of things, but seemed to have terrible difficulty, sometimes, in making up his mind when faced with a problem or a decision that had to be taken. At this moment Cosmo began to see why. Fancy growing up with a thing like that hanging over you, he thought. And then: now it's hanging over *me*. He wrapped his arms tightly round his knees.

"No," Eunice agreed. "He should have told your mother before he married her. Given her the chance to cry off."

"Did she find out? In the end?"

"Yes."

"How?"

"*I* told her," Cousin Eunice said, still with that undertone of violence. "There were Mark and you growing up—I thought she ought to know."

"I see." Cosmo did not, in fact, wholly see; he guessed there had been anger, a quarrel, bitterness. "Did you *like* my mother?" he asked timidly.

"She was my greatest friend in the world. We were at college together. That was how she came to meet Dick— your father."

There was silence for a while. They both gazed at the fire. Mrs Tydings's needles clicked. Then Cosmo said,

"Did it always—? I mean: sometimes there must have been Curtoyses who didn't marry, or didn't have sons—?"

"Oh yes, sometimes. Sometimes, perhaps, people chose not to have children. But there was always a younger brother somewhere— Anyway, that was why, when your mother heard what she was very likely in for—first she persuaded your father to move to Australia— she said that was a good long way off from any war that was likely to break out."

"They always die in *battle*?"

"Yes, in battle, fighting. And then something must have made your mother realize that running away wasn't going to solve the problem—"

"She talked to an aborigine sorcerer," Cosmo said absently. He remembered the impressive old man who had

48

come past their house, one dry spring day, and Ma had offered him a drink of iced tea and some fruit, and they had started talking. She had never been the same after that ...

"I suppose he must have told her that you can't get away from your ancestors," Cousin Eunice said thoughtfully. "Did he tell *you* anything, Cosmo?"

"Yes, he told me that I would have three friends." Rather a boring prediction, tossed off as if the old fellow wanted to be kind to the younger brother, but couldn't think of anything more interesting to say. He had told Mark – what had he told Mark? – something about battles, that was it – that there were many different kinds.

"What do you think *happened* to Mother and Mark?" Cosmo said to Cousin Eunice.

"My dear, I doubt if we shall ever know."

"You don't think they could – could still be alive?"

"In the middle of that desert? When they had left their car and walked – no, my dear. It's just not possible. You mustn't waste yourself hoping for a miracle. I'm afraid you – we – just have to accept that they chose to opt out. They were very, very fond of each other. *I* think it was very tough on you – and on Richard. But *I* can't judge them. All I can say is, I wouldn't have done it like that."

"Nor you wouldn't have gone to Australia," Mrs Tydings observed, twining two ends of wool together.

"No. Well. People are different. So – so now you know what your problem is, Cosmo. And you've got time to decide how to deal with it. You could decide not to marry – or not to have children."

"That might be best. But I could adopt some, I suppose – *they* wouldn't be under the curse?"

"Not a bad idea. I don't see why they should."

"Does the curse go on for ever?"

"I don't know enough about curses to answer that."

"Do you *believe* in curses, Cousin Eunice?"

"Well, we must, mustn't we? In view of the evidence. I expect," she said, frowning thoughtfully, "that it was a case of vibrations. Something we don't understand much about yet, like radiation. Think what a fearfully powerful force that is—one little piece of plutonium can change whole landscapes and generations. Well, this must be something similar. And it has really affected the genes of the Curtoys family. Maybe it takes something equally drastic to get it out—a kind of mutation. If you know what that is."

"A variation from your ancestral type."

"Hey—those bush correspondence courses must have been pretty good."

Suddenly Cosmo felt exceedingly tired. He wanted to get away and think over all that he had been told.

"Let's wash up," he said, "and then I reckon I'll go to bed."

"Never mind about the washing up, my lamb," Mrs Tydings said. "That'll wait over till the morning. You take yourself off and have a nice hot bath—get the smell of school off you."

School! He had forgotten all about the place. It seemed a thousand miles away.

"Goodnight, Cosmo," Cousin Eunice said. Unexpectedly, she gave him a brief hug, and added, "Don't start worrying too much, if you can help it. Things always turn out differently from what you expect."

"And *that's* true," said Mrs Tydings.

Cosmo went up to his room. But he did not immediately go to bed. He leaned on the low windowsill looking out, listening to a screech-owl going whit-whit-whit, and the river sighing to itself in the distance, and the vague mutter of the weir. Strange to think of ancient Britons in a temple somewhere up in the woods – perhaps where Mr Marvell had been ploughing the chocolate earth with Prince and Blossom; the river and the screech-owl must have sounded just the same then. Two thousand years wasn't so very long ago when you thought of the Pleistocene Age.

At last he stepped back from the window, and, as he did so, something whitish, and about the size of half a banana fell out of his jacket sleeve on to the floor. What in the world could it have been? A tissue, a bit of Mrs Tydings's wool? He switched on his table-lamp and put it down on the mat, but the thing seemed to have vanished totally. Could it have blown away? Or *run*? It must have been his imagination, but it had seemed to scurry off under the desk as if it had embryonic legs – like a white lizard. But there were no lizards in England – not that size, anyway, or at this time of year – and anyway, how could it have been *up his sleeve*? He must have imagined the whole incident.

I'm tired, he told himself, and bothered by all that stuff about the curse – can Cousin Eunice seriously believe it? I'll have my bath and go to bed.

He had his bath and got into bed. He wrote in his diary, "Cousin Eunice told me about the family Curse." He put the light out and shut his eyes. But his mind went on working. Because, firstly, it was plain that Cousin Eunice *did* believe in the curse; and so did Mrs Tydings; and so, for that matter, did he; and secondly he knew that he had not imagined the white thing that fell out of his sleeve.

So where could it be?

3

Little Con

STEPPING OUT OF THE Rolls into the Woodstock Road on Monday morning, Cosmo found it hard to take school very seriously. He had done all his homework – written a pretty good piece on Roman Britain, actually – but, apart from that, the weekend had been a million light-years removed from school. Despite Eunice's amazing revelations and the shadow of the family curse, the two days had been full of good activities. Mr Marvell had taught Cosmo how to use the harrow, and he had been introduced to the foals of Blossom and Duchess, and allowed to choose names for them – he had chosen Juno and Punch; Mr Marvell had also found him some steel pitons, and he had started the long, tough job of hammering them into the walnut trunk to make a spiral stair. So far he had put in three; it was not a job you could work at for very long at a stretch. And he had begun to make a camp on the island among the elder trees which had grown up into a forest, and had helped Cousin Eunice lay a paved path with big slabs of Oxfordshire stone along by the yew hedge. And he had written a long letter to his father, whom he wanted to talk to very badly indeed

– though it certainly was going to be strange meeting him again with all this stuff about the curse between them. Poor Dad, Cosmo thought; he must feel terribly lonely over there, waiting for the man to come and take over his practice; waiting for news that won't come. Mark and Ma were always the ones who were close together; now I understand why Father used to look so sad and left-out sometimes. I wonder if I shall ever feel like that?

Does it make it easier, knowing that something is bound to happen? Or does it make it worse?

Occupied with these ideas, he walked into school, and the atmosphere suddenly hit him like a bucketful of salt water in the face.

For a start, it seemed that, all of a sudden, everybody in his form hated him.

"Oh cripes, look who's here," Charley groaned, as he walked into the Remove room.

"Oh-oh," said somebody else. "The Boy Wonder is with us again. Our hero of the kangaroos."

Cosmo pretended he hadn't heard these remarks, and dumped his homework exercise books on the piles laid out to be collected.

But as the day wore on he could not pretend to ignore the hostility any more. It was too open. People continually made sour or sharp remarks, obviously aimed at him; everything he said was greeted with acid comment or withering silence; people ostentatiously moved away from him as if he were contagious.

"What the dickens *is* all this?" he was finally provoked into saying. "What's the matter, have I got the plague, or something?"

"No," said Charley coldly, "we have just decided that you are disgustingly stuck up, and that as well as being a swank you are a liar and a cheat. So we just don't want to have anything more to do with you than we absolutely have to. You're lucky actually – last year, when we were in third Preparatory, we'd probably have hung you upside down by your feet out of the window; but this year as we are halfway up the school, we've decided just to send you to Coventry."

"Gee, thanks!" He was so angry, that was all he could say for a minute or two; then, sickened at the sight of all their smug, waiting faces, he burst out, "What the blazes do you *mean*, I'm a liar and a cheat? I am *not*!"

"You cheated at Dodge-ball. We all saw you."

"I did not! Anyway, everybody cheats. I saw a lot of you cheating," he said, fatally weakening his case.

"And you've told a whole lot of lies about Australia. For all we know, you've never even been there. In fact, nobody here believes a single word you say."

"Too bad," he said coldly.

"So we've decided we aren't going to speak to you any more – except in lessons or when we absolutely have to."

"I doubt if I'll miss your charming conversation! Good grief, how childish can you get," he muttered. "And how long, might I ask, do you intend to keep that up?"

Nobody answered.

The day thus badly begun went on worse. He had done the wrong lot of maths prep ("Just to show off," somebody whispered), and he got a black mark for that, and another for going across the garden in the rain without his raincoat. The lessons were a strain, since he knew that, if he answered a question, somebody would be sure to murmur, "Swank! Know-all!" and if he said he didn't know, the teachers would think he was a dumb fool. In between lessons, he had to endure all the pointed remarks aimed at him.

"Too bad there isn't room for you at this table, Meredith. It's pretty hard on you having to sit at a table with that pair of smelly dumbheads."

"It's going to be awkward when the autumn term comes and we have to split up for studies. Who'd want to share a study with *him*?"

"Gabby will have to find him a special room by himself."

"Even Bun wouldn't want to share with him – would you, Bun?"

"N-No," said poor Bun, and gave Cosmo a nervous, propitiating look.

The Intermediate forms, Cosmo had already learned, to mark their advance into the upper school, were given the privilege of small, cell-like studies, which were shared between three or four people; he had observed that, months ahead, the social problem of who was going to share with whom was a matter of terrific importance, much discussion, and a lot of careful, anxious arrangement, since, once you were fixed up in a study with somebody, it was not easy to change, unless one of you left the school. So you might find yourself, up at Senior level, cumbered with some ninny who had seemed congenial when you were younger; or you might, in your haste to get yourself respectably paired off, not left out in the cold, snatch the first offer, and so miss the person or people you would really have liked to share with. Cosmo had already wondered rather apprehensively who his study-mates were likely to be. Charley and Moley would obviously share with each other, and probably with the other boy, Chris, who went round with them a good deal; Andy and Lot would probably join up with Rebecca, they seemed to like the big cheerful German girl and all shared an interest in stamp-collecting, of all boring things; Sheil, Tansy and Meredith might all go together; that left him the dismal prospect of sharing with Bun. But suppose even Bun wouldn't have him?

"*He'll* never find three friends to share with," Charley remarked, as if listening to Cosmo's thought. "I'm afraid poor old Cosmo Curt-oise will have to go up in the attic by himself."

"What a name to be saddled with," giggled Tansy – for such a giggly girl, she was very spiteful, as Cosmo had already discovered. "Cosmo! It sounds like cough mixture."

"Cosmic. Comic. Comic Curt-oise."

"Hey, Comic? How d'you like Morningquest School?"

"I thought you weren't supposed to be speaking to me," Cosmo said sourly.

He looked at their hostile, mocking faces, and hated the lot of them – supercilious, freckled Charley, sycophantic Moley, dull, self-satisfied Andy and Lot, dumb Rebecca, surly Chris, spiteful Tansy, stupid Bun, moody cross-eyed Sheil, and cool sarcastic Meredith. How in heaven's name was he going to put up with a week of this? A week, a month, a term?

It went on, and it grew worse. During prayers everybody in the form shuffled about, making it plain that they were trying to avoid standing next to Cosmo, until sharply reprimanded by Mr Cheevy; at meals his own form kept well away from him; in football the boys refused to pass to him, even when he was well-placed for a pass, although they were bawled out for this by Mr Breadbury; and, at other times, such as eleven o'clock break, when everybody was supposed to go out into the garden, he was left conspicuously alone and had to walk round by himself; he stuck his hands in his pockets, hunched his head between his shoulders, and tried to look as if he had a tremendous lot on his mind, maybe working out the theory of relativity. Well, he *had* a lot on his mind, damn it! Little did those dumb oafs know what problems he had to worry about. Anyway, that was one thing he would never, never tell them; for if he breathed a single word about the family curse, they would be certain to label it both outrageous swank *and* lying to get attention — as if he wanted their horrible attention! As a matter of fact, compared with this sudden and disconcerting unpopularity, the thought of the Curtoys Curse was almost comfortable, and at least interesting; certainly thinking about it took his mind off his present troubles. And he thought about it a great deal in the course of the week. There were all kinds of things he wanted to ask Eunice — for instance, had Father talked to her about it when they were young together at Courtoys Place? Had she known about it then? At what stage had Mark been told, as he obviously had; and why was Mark told when he, Cosmo, had been kept in the dark?

Perhaps some new boys would come to the school in the autumn term — or girls — and he could share a study with them.

Or perhaps Father would decide not to come to England after all, and would summon Cosmo back to Australia. It would certainly be good to leave this hateful, spiteful school, but as against that, he already felt rooted in at the mill house, with Eunice and Mrs Tydings; he really didn't want to leave it. If only he didn't have to go to school!

Midway through the week — which went on just as badly as it had started — Mr Gabbitas sent for him again.

"Poor old Comic's going to cry his eyes out on Gabby's lap," whispered Tansy audibly to Rebecca, who laughed heartily.

"Well, Cosmo, how is it going?" inquired Mr Gabbitas with that sweet smile which crinkled up his eyes but didn't seem to get to the middle of them. "Feeling more settled, are you? Making friends, hmn? Mr Cheevy seemed to think that you were looking a little troubled – any problems bothering you that I can help you sort out?"

Well, sir, I've just heard about this ancestral curse, and as well as that my form has decided, for no particular reason, to send me to Coventry. And a nasty little white thing like an outsize tadpole fell out of my sleeve and I haven't seen it since, and the thought of it keeps bothering me, I can't help wondering where it got to.

"No, thank you, I'm quite all right," he said. "Sir."

"It does take a while getting used to a new place," said Mr Gabbitas. "I daresay in a couple of months' time you'll look back and be quite amazed at how differently you feel about things."

"Yes sir," said Cosmo politely.

"Not finding the work too hard, eh? Mr Cheevy reports that you are well up to your age level – in fact rather *beyond* it here and there – still, I expect the others have plenty to teach you in different ways?"

"Yes, they do."

Mr Gabbitas sighed. "Very well, Cosmo, run along then."

Outside the door he found the pale Meredith waiting her turn to see the headmaster.

She, at first, had seemed a good deal more sensible than some of the others in the form, and on an impulse he said to her quietly, "I say, isn't this Coventry business a bit stupid?"

She shrugged her shoulders and answered in a toneless little voice,

"Everyone has to go through it when they're new. We all did. It's supposed to help you find your level." And she went on into Mr Gabbitas's study.

"Ah, Meredith," the headmaster said, much more warmly than he had to Cosmo; then the door shut.

After lunch, between half-past one and two, people were allowed, if they had any pocket-money, to buy chocolate and sweets from a store presided over by silly Miss Gracie the music mistress. In Australia, Cosmo had never eaten sweets, but now he had a sudden passionate craving for things that were chewy and gooey, Mars bars, Crunchies, whipped-cream walnuts. Eunice had given him a pound for pocket-money, so he went up to Miss Gracie's cupboard after lunch and bought three Mars bars.

"Getting some for your friends too, are you?" smiled Miss Gracie—obviously it hadn't occurred to her that a person could eat three Mars bars all by himself. Cosmo heard Chris murmur to Charley in the line behind,

"What a hope! He must be going to guzzle them all on his own. I don't suppose Comic Curtoise has a single friend in this hemisphere."

"As a matter of fact you couldn't be more wrong," remarked Cosmo coldly, surprising even himself. "I have three friends out at my cousin's place, which is why I don't give a rap whether any of you stuck-up lot speak to me or not."

"Just imagine! He has three whole friends! And what might be the names of these lucky, lucky persons?"

"Percy, Bert and Oscar." Where had those names come from? They had flashed into his head like lightning. But they had the wrong effect on Chris and Charley, who fell about laughing.

"Percy—Bert—and *Oscar*! Oh, hold me up, someone! Percy the Penguin. Burlington Bertie, the Kernel of the Nuts. And Oscar! What about Cedric? What about little Lord Fauntleroy? Isn't he there?"

59

"Move along, move along, please," said Miss Gracie, getting flustered. "You're holding up the line."

Chris and Charley followed Cosmo downstairs.

"I suppose you and Percy and dear Bertie and Ossie all play ring-a-roses with that nice lady who brings you in the Rolls. Your aunt, is she?"

"No, as a matter of fact she's a vampire—she's Dracula's aunt."

Chris and Charley looked at one another solemnly. "Oh-oh. Wonder Boy's getting uppish."

Cosmo left them abruptly and walked away towards the cloakrooms. As he went, he heard them reporting the exchange to Moley, and Moley's sudden engaging bubble of laughter. "I say, Dracula's Aunt—that's rather good!"

Cosmo locked himself in the loo, intending to eat one of his Mars bars, but was confronted by a pencilled notice on the wall that said, "Cosmo Curtoys is a Swanky Ass".

He suddenly felt sick, and discovered that chocolate was the last thing he wanted.

By Friday, when Eunice came to fetch him, he still had not eaten the Mars bars.

The nickname Dracula's Aunt had somehow stuck to her. People said to each other, "I say, do you know that Cosmo Curtoys lives with Dracula's Aunt? He has a nice basin of blood for breakfast every Saturday." This had gone the rounds of the lower forms, and by four o'clock on Friday afternoon quite a number of people were hanging about the front steps, interested to see the Rolls and its driver. Lob was in the car too—he came in on Fridays as Eunice spent only half a day in college; somebody murmured, "There's Dracula's dachshund."

Eunice—who had come straight from a lecture and was

still wearing her black gown—looked keenly at the assembled spectators, and said,

"Hullo! Could somebody tell Cosmo Curtoys that I'm here for him, please?"

But at that moment Cosmo himself came out of the door with his duffel-bag and got into the car.

"Goodbye," Eunice said politely to the watchers on the threshold. A faint cheer of hip-hip-hurray went up as the Rolls crunched out of the gateway.

"Were those friends or enemies?" Eunice asked.

"Enemies."

"Heavens. You certainly seem to have made plenty." She sounded quite calm about it. "What did you do—fight them all?"

"No, they just sort of—sort of appointed themselves."

"Oh well, if it happened as unreasonably as that, they'll probably *dis*-appoint themselves equally fast.—It's tough while it lasts though. How's work going?"

He started telling her, and she asked a number of questions about his science and maths which made the journey home pass in a flash.

Cosmo felt peculiarly nervous when he first went up to his bedroom; try as he would, he couldn't get out of his mind the memory of that little whitish thing. In the course of last weekend he had hunted for it very thoroughly several times, and found nothing, but the room was old and cornery—in fact it had a small square trap-door in one corner that led straight into the roof—there were lots of places where the thing could have hidden itself, a cupboard that held a water-tank, and the huge wardrobe at the end of the room.

"Are there rats here?" he asked Eunice, who said,

"Why? Did you hear scurryings in the roof? Starlings,

more likely; or mice. Lob wouldn't allow rats; he keeps the place clear of them. But he despises mice; they could sit on his feet and he wouldn't bother."

Lob was very fond of chocolate, and Cosmo had the idea of enticing the old dog up to his room with crumbs of Mars bar, but the result was rather disconcerting: Lob stopped in the doorway, growling deep in his throat, with the fur on his shoulders all ruffled up, and flatly refused to come inside. Then, ignoring offers of more bits of Mars, he turned round and hurried away down the wide, polished stairs with his toenails rattling and his tail between his legs.

However, despite another very careful search, Cosmo could see nothing in the room. He decided to sit down and do his prep at once, get it over with. These days the evenings were growing lighter; it would not be dark until seven. Eunice was outside the house, mowing the lawn; he could see her, each time she came across. Her pale hair was tied back with a handkerchief and she wore an old pair of corduroys all stained with green. She was a reassuring sight.

He opened the window and called, "Shall I help?"

"Get your work done first. There's plenty of grass!"

He had laid the three Mars bars in a row on his bed. He intended to eat them at the rate of one a day over the weekend: the first, what was left of it, tonight after supper, while reading *Flatland*, an extraordinary book that Eunice had given him; the second tomorrow while doing farm-work, maybe Mr Marvell would share it; and, if he got all his pitons hammered in, the third up in the fork of the walnut tree on Sunday.

With this planned in his mind, he settled down to work. Maths first, then a description of an experiment done to prove that potatoes contain starch, fairly elementary stuff; then an essay about the Silk Route; quite interesting, that was, he became really absorbed in it, only noticing, with about an eighth of his attention, how the sound of the mower became gradually louder as Eunice worked her way back and forth across the lawn, slowly coming closer to the house.

At last he had finished, and stood up, stretching his stiff writing-fingers. Eight pages! Even sour-faced Cheevy ought to be satisfied with that.

There was still a third of the lawn left to mow, he saw; he could go out now and take over from Eunice. He turned to leave the room – and stood still in shock. For, as he moved, the draught from his movement, or perhaps from the open window, caused the three Mars bar wrappers to flutter from the bed to the floor. The wrappers were empty – the contents were gone! What was even more extraordinary, he found, as he picked them up – first looking sharply about the room and under the bed – was that the two unopened wrappers were *still* unopened, square and tidy, the ends neatly sealed, just as they had come from the factory – only they were hollow, there was nothing inside. Not a crumb of chocolate remained. Rather wildly, Cosmo began hunting about the room again – under the bed, in the cupboards, the wardrobe, his empty suitcases. Then, while he had his back half turned from the window, something caught his eye, a flash of movement, and he spun round, just too late to see exactly what it was that had scrabbled over the sill. He bounded across the room and leaned out of the window. There was a sloping roof down below, over a kind of garden-room, running the length of the house, where tools and deckchairs were kept. A useful emergency exit from his room, he had already decided, since the drop from the edge of the roof to the ground was only about seven feet; now it seemed that something else had had the same idea. Whatever it had been was already out of sight. Thinking that he might intercept it if he went the other way, Cosmo raced down the stairs and out the side door. He ran round the side of the house to where Eunice was still mowing.

"D'you want to take over now?" she said.

"Yes, okay. — Eunice, did you see anything come out of my window?"

"What sort of thing?"

He explained about the Mars bars — rather embarrassed by them, but she didn't say "Greedy pig" or anything like that, only remarked, "It might have been a squirrel. They are terrible thieves, and they do get into the house sometimes; Emma lost a whole batch of quince jelly she'd left on the windowsill to cool last year."

Cosmo thought about the half-glimpse he'd had of the escaping creature. No, he was sure it couldn't have been a squirrel — it was too big, for a start. And too pale in colour — sallow, greyish white. He couldn't help feeling sure that it was the thing that had come out of his sleeve — only now it had grown. Unless it was another of the same kind, larger. This had been about the size of a cat or rabbit — as far as he could judge out of the corner of his eye. And there was something about its shape — tapering like a tadpole — or a fish — or like some rather beastly pictures that hung in the school dining-room, pink people like sardines gazing up at God. By William Blake. They gave him the gooeys.

All this went through his mind fast. He decided that he could not — *definitely* could not – tell Cousin Eunice any more about the white thing. It had been too disgusting. Anyway – whatever it was — had left the house now. That, at least, was something to be thankful for, he thought, taking the warm handles of the mower and beginning to guide it across the grass. Should he have shut his window? But very likely

64

the thing wouldn't be able to climb back in again, because of the drop from the edge of the roof to the ground. You'd need to be pretty athletic to get up there. And it hadn't looked athletic—not at all. More like a horrible little embryo.

"Has this house ever been haunted?" he asked in a careless manner at supper.

"Are you thinking that a ghost might have made off with your chocolate?" said Eunice laughing.

"Haunted? This house? Never!" declared Mrs Tydings with great firmness. "And *I* ought to know, for my uncle Sid was the miller here, when I was scullerymaid up at the Place at age twelve; no one's ever heard of a ghost here. Not *in* the house, that's to say—o' course there's the coach-and-six that drives past the gate at full moon—but that's never been known to stop, anyway."

"A *coach-and-six*? Are you kidding?"

"Certainly not!" She was affronted. "I've seen it meself, time-and-again—mostly when I was took bad with the indigestion, and had to get up in the night for a bit of bicarb—" with a sniff of a chuckle. "Three o'clock or thereabouts it's supposed to pass by; yes, I've seen it plain enough. It goes along where the old road used to run; by the side of the meddar and then round the edge of the wood. You can see it easy from my upstairs windows."

"Have *you* seen it, Cousin Eunice?"

Eunice answered vaguely and exasperatingly that she thought she had, but couldn't be positive. "It's one of those muddly memories—you don't know if you really saw something, or only intended to. Your father and I always *meant* to get up at half-past two and come down here from the Place to watch for it; only now I'm not certain whether we ever did or not."

The tale of the coach-and-six somehow cheered Cosmo very much. That was a proper kind of ghost – he could hardly withhold a grin as he wondered how his enemies in Remove would react to that, if he told them about it. More lying, they would label it, doubtless, more swank and romancing. He certainly intended to try and see the coach himself – full moon wasn't for several weeks, there had just been one. He resolved not to miss the next opportunity.

And somehow, oddly, the thought of the phantom coach made the other thing easier to take.

But still he hoped very much that it would not come back. It was welcome to his Mars bars.

On Saturday Mr Marvell showed Cosmo how to run the electric milker. He was made to take a lot of stringent precautions before being allowed into the milking-shed, wading in his wellingtons through a trough of disinfectant, putting on clean overalls: "Against bovine tuberculosis, that is," said Mr Marvell, who was very sold on hygiene – and washing his hands and arms most thoroughly before putting on rubber gloves – but it was worth all the trouble, for the little Channel Island cows were so charming – Cherry, Merry, Kerry, Berry, Perry, and Sherry – with their silky mouse-coloured coats and great black-ringed eyes and elegant scooped-out faces. They all had to be shampooed before milking and were so clean and sleek that he felt they ought to come into the house and sit in a ring round the fire like Lob. They were hardly bigger than the dog, it seemed amazing that they could produce all that creamy milk.

After milking, Cosmo worked on his island camp, making a palisade of elder branches round it, and cutting down a lot of nettles that were sprouting fast. He could not withstand the fidgety feeling, while so occupied, that something was watching him: every now and then he heard a rustle among the undergrowth; but whatever it was never came into view. An otter, perhaps?

Then he hammered six more pitons into the walnut trunk. He was getting quite high by now, working round in a spiral, spacing them about two-foot-six apart. It was a particularly hellish job. Mr Marvell had kindly lent him a drill to start the holes, which was some help – but even so the walnut trunk was formidably hard with greyish wrinkled bark like the hide of a prehistoric hippopotamus. Being obliged to drill and then hammer while precariously balanced on a lower piton was very bad; if he used both hands, to hold the piton and to hammer, he unbalanced himself and fell off; while if he used only one and hung on with the other, then the piton tended to fall out and he had to climb down and fetch it, cursing. He had tried Eunice's fruit-ladder but it unfortunately wasn't high enough. His arms and legs ached like blazes – the muscles were being worked to death. Two more pitons would be enough, he decided – now he was almost within reach of the fork.

Mr Marvell passed by, on his way to inspect the water-meadows for sogginess; he tested a couple of the lower pitons, and said that Cosmo was making a gradely job of it – gradely was his highest term of praise.

Dusk was falling, and Cosmo had almost made up his mind to leave the final piton for Sunday morning, when a little shrill whining voice from below, at the foot of the tree, caused him to start so violently that he almost fell, and dropped the last piton with a clang.

The voice cried, peevishly, "Lemme up too! Con wants to come! Lemme up, lemme up!"

"Who the *devil* are *you*? And where did you come from?" Cosmo croaked, when he had recovered his voice.

Down at the foot of the tree was a horrible little boy –

aged four or five, perhaps? Cosmo had never had anything to do with younger children, so he didn't know – jigging fretfully up and down, clutching the lowest piton, which was just within his reach, and whining like a gnat, "Lemme up! Not fair leave Con out! Connie come up too!"

Cosmo was immensely thankful that he had deliberately placed the lowest piton quite high up, so that only a long-legged, agile person could start the climb. This monstrous little imp couldn't make it, that was for sure. Could he be something to do with Mr Marvell – a nephew, grandchild, friend's child?

Mrs Tydings came from the house with a basketful of teacloths to peg on the line, and Cosmo shouted to her,

"Hey, where did this one come from?"

Then he got another bad shock. For she replied, "What's that, dear?" and walked right past, without appearing to notice the little monster wailing and hopping up and down.

"Why *him*! That beastly little brat!"

"Brat, what brat?"

"That boy!"

"There's no boy about, dear," she replied, and passed so close to the kid that she could have knocked him over with her basket.

Cosmo came slowly down the trunk until he was on the bottom-but-one piton, where he stopped, taking a good look at the child. He saw a small stocky boy, pudgy-faced, with short dirty fair curls, a scowling pugnacious expression, dressed in grubby ragged clothes that were much too small for him – he resembled somebody – who could it be? Brown goo was smeared round his mouth and over his cheeks. The reason for *that* flashed upon Cosmo at the same time as he noticed something else odd about the kid's appearance: he flickered. He came and went like a faulty film, or the sound of a radio station that isn't properly tuned; although shaped so solidly, he quivered on the air as if printed on a screen that wasn't quite there. Cosmo had seen an exhibition of holographs once in Sydney—pictures written on the air with laser beams. They *seemed* quite real, three-dimensional, yet they were just an effect of light. So with this little monster.

"You're nothing but a beastly spook!" Cosmo snapped at him. "So how the devil could you eat my Mars bars? You little thief!"

"Connie wanna come up too! Lift Connie up!"

Secretly, Cosmo had always wanted a younger brother. Mark had been the leader since before Cosmo was born— the hero, somebody to admire and follow, superior in every way. It would have been a great comfort to have someone smaller as well, somebody to protect and instruct and boss a bit, a person who would look up to him as he looked up to Mark. It was still very much a part of his hollow, sad, resentful feeling against Mark and Ma that, by going off together like that—*deserting* him—they had also robbed him of the chance of a younger brother. But *he* would have been quite different from this horrible little creature.

"Get away from here—buzz off!" he called down. "You don't belong here."

"Connie come up! Lemme come up too."

"*No!* You're much too small."

The ache in Cosmo's arms, hanging on the piton all this time, had become nearly unbearable. He would have to jump down. And it would certainly be shameful to show fear of a brat half his size.

Cousin Eunice put her head out of the open kitchen window and swung the dinner bell.

"Cosmo! Supper's ready!"

"Coming!" he called back, and jumped. And when he hit the ground, there was no child to be seen. It was as if the shock-wave from Cosmo's landing had jiggled him out of existence, dissolved him back to some other plane.

At supper Cosmo was rather silent. But that was all right; nobody expected him to talk if he did not feel like it. Mrs Tydings was talking about spring-cleaning the attics, and Eunice, in between spells of brooding about a lecture that she was constructing, talked about the book *Flatland*.

"It's meant to be a satire," she explained, "like *Gulliver's Travels*. The idea of people living in a two-dimensional world, perfectly satisfied with having just length and breadth, and quite unable to imagine height. What the author means to suggest is that *we* are just the same—all we know about is our three dimensions, and we are quite positive that there can't be a fourth."

"Yes, I see."

"And of course the author pokes fun at other things along the way. Like the women in Flatland, for instance, who are just straight lines, pointed at each end." Eunice picked up the book and read. "'Place a needle on the table. Look at it end-ways, and you see nothing but a point: it has become practically invisible. Just so is it with one of our Women. When the end containing her eye or mouth—for with us these organs are identical—is the part that meets our eye, then we see nothing but a highly lustrous point. The dangers to which we are exposed from our Women must now be manifest to the meanest capacity;—what can it be to run against a Woman except absolute and immediate destruction!' ... So the Flatlanders have special laws for women, that when they are walking in a public place they must constantly keep up a Peace-Cry, and that any woman suffering from violent sneezing or St Vitus' Dance must be instantly destroyed. — And then there are all the penalties suffered by the Irregulars. There the author is making fun of the way that society as a whole always turns against people who don't conform to all its rules. — 'Doubtless the life of an Irregular is hard, but the interests of the Greater Number require that it *shall* be hard. If a man with a triangular front and a polygonal back were allowed to propagate a still more Irregular posterity, what would become of the arts of life? Are the houses and doors and churches in Flatland to be altered to accommodate such monsters?'" Eunice chuckled, and gave the book back to Cosmo.

"People are just like that everywhere. If you are a different shape, they send you to prison, or say you are mad, or, like the Flatlanders, shut you up in a government office as a clerk of the seventh class."

"Cousin Eunice, do you believe that there are dimensions we don't know about?"

"Oh, sure to be. Why should we assume that we know everything there is to be known? Well, we know that we *don't*, because we keep discovering new things all the time, like Black Holes in space, or the fact that some molecules seem to be magnetized."

"Well then — if there *are* other dimensions — can there be some connection between what is happening in them — and us?"

"How do you mean, exactly?"

"Well — well, that coach-and-six that passes the gate when the moon is full — that could be something that's happening in another dimension, right? We just happen to see it because there's a fold in space at that point — or in time — it happened a couple of hundred years ago, but because of the fold it keeps coming back again — like a stuck gramophone record?"

"Something of the kind."

"Well," he said, "can we get *in touch* with the coach?"

"You mean, can we affect what happens in other dimensions? Or can those happenings affect us?"

"Yes."

"I honestly don't see why not," said Eunice thoughtfully. "After all, even if you just see a thing, it can affect you in all kinds of ways – frighten you, or make you laugh, or make you sad. Seeing a film can change your life. And if the sight of a thing can do that to you, then the sight of *you* can affect *it*. There's a theory, you know, that no experiment can be wholly detached and scientific if somebody is observing it. 'Dear sir, it is not at all odd, *I* am always about in the quad, And that's why the tree, Still continues to be, In the sight of, Yours faithfully, God!'"

"It's high time that boy was in bed," said Mrs Tydings, bustling about and whipping a plate from under Cosmo's elbow. "He's got great black circles under his eyes. Reading in bed till all hours, I daresay! That's what comes of giving them bedside lamps. I saw your light last night, shining at eleven! Let's see it go out a bit earlier tonight."

"Just one minute more! We might see the coach because somebody is sending the image of it to us?"

"Yes, people have done experiments along those lines, and got quite positive results. Sending images of screwdrivers and things like that. Some people are very strong Senders. There was a man in Chicago who could actually put a mental image on to a Polaroid film."

"Okay, let's wash the dishes," said Cosmo jumping up.

He went to sleep that night as soon as his head hit the pillow. He was really tired out. But next day he hammered in his last piton, and began the construction of a platform in the walnut tree.

He had no glimpse of little Con all day—which was a considerable relief, he couldn't help admitting to himself—but, over and over, had the feeling that he was being watched, as he had in the island camp.

On Monday morning, just as he was getting into the Rolls to go off with Eunice, Lob, who was sitting on the big stone slab outside the front door, suddenly let out a low growl and retired into the house.

"What's up, Lobby?" said Eunice, who was checking in her briefcase that she had her lecture notes and Mrs Tydings's shopping list. "It's only the post. Good morning, Tad."

"Morning, Miss Eunice. There's a letter for the young feller from Australia."

"Reward for starting late," said Eunice. "Five minutes earlier and you wouldn't have had it till Friday."

Cosmo was happy to have his father's letter but didn't open it right away.

"Eunice," he said, "can you see anybody in the cartshed?"

She glanced over her shoulder—she was in the middle of backing and turning the car. "No, why?"

"Nothing—I thought—but it's gone."

He had seen a boy of about his own height—fair—angry-looking, as if he were annoyed that they were going off without him. He was holding a hayfork and had a pile of sacking or tarpaulin over his arm. Then he moved and vanished; Cosmo remembered the description of the needle turning endways in Flatland. It was a similar process. He turned sideways and disappeared, as if into a vertical crack in the air beside him. As he did so, Cosmo realized why his face seemed so familiar—he was the boy who had come to help with damming the brook, all those years ago. That was who he was! Only then he had seemed bigger—perhaps because Cosmo himself had been smaller ...

"Sorry," he said, stirring himself free from his thoughts and jumping out to open the gate. He waited till the Rolls had slipped through, then shut it again.

But was *that* boy the same as yesterday's hateful little four-year-old? They had a resemblance. Was Cosmo getting glimpses of him at different ages? Was he *growing*?

And, if so, what size would he be by next weekend?

"What does Dick have to say?" asked Eunice, skirting round one of the many potholes.

"Hopes to get here some time in July. He's found somebody to take over the practice and buy the house – " Cosmo gulped a little, thinking of that house. It had been nothing out of the common, built of wood, with a corrugated roof, but it had been spacious and comfortable, they had lived in it for six years, collected a lot of things together, played games, learned lessons, talked and argued. It had been their home. Now strangers would be living in it who knew nothing about them – looking out of Ma's kitchen window, leaning on the wall that Mark had built.

"That's fine," Eunice said. She asked no more questions, and Cosmo decided to leave the rest of his father's letter until later in the day. It was hard reading in the car. Richard's writing was spiky and difficult to decipher.

Cosmo had been apprehensive that there might be a reception committee there on the steps ready to greet him with groans, and Eunice with cries of "Dracula's Aunt", but of course on Monday morning everybody was in too much of a rush for anything of that kind.

He said, "Goodbye, thank you for a lovely weekend."

"See you on Friday," she called, and had slipped over the turnaround and out into the Woodstock Road traffic before he was up the front steps.

4

Big Con

SCHOOL THAT WEEK WAS nasty, but not unbearable. For one thing, some of the lessons were turning out to be downright interesting. And then, though Cosmo's form were still ostentatiously ostracizing him, he had at least plenty to be thinking about. Also he had invented a method for keeping calm during the break period when he had to walk round the garden by himself like a leper. This was to imagine that his brother Mark was with him, and that he was filling Mark in on all that had happened to him since he came to England.

"Seeing ghosts?" he imagined Mark saying rather sceptically. Mark had never been one to believe anything unless the proof of it was demonstrated right under his nose.

Or had he?

"Well, *you* ran off into the desert because of a curse," Cosmo retorted. "What's the difference between that and seeing ghosts?"

"I *chose* to go off into the desert because I didn't choose to die in some stupid war," Mark answered haughtily. "Wars are an outdated way of settling problems."

Father had written something of the kind in his letter.

"You and I are faced with the same enigma, Cosmo," he had written. "Eunice phoned me that she had told you about the family ill-wish thing. Whether it really works or not isn't the point. Obviously if someone believes that it is going to work, it will, for them. And it's plain that Mark and your mother did believe; or, at least, they weren't taking any chances. Now you and I have got to try to *forgive* them for making that decision – for going off without us. And that may be terribly hard, but it's crucially necessary. It's no use having bitter feelings against people – specially people who are gone – it's as bad as going round all the time hitting yourself over the head with a brick. Anyway I hope the school Eunice chose for you is providing plenty of interesting distraction. And I'm glad to think of you at the mill house with Eunice and old Mrs T. That place, and those two, should help you to feel better about your problems."

"And may provide a few more," Cosmo couldn't help thinking.

He folded up the letter – which he had been reading for the seventh time – and turned to go into the school building. A bell was ringing for the end of break.

Climbing the iron steps, he was just ahead of a black-haired boy from the Senior class – the same one who had been sent on his first day to fetch him to the headmaster's study. Cosmo now knew that he was one of the two headboys and that his name was Roger Maugham.

"Hullo," he greeted Cosmo with easy friendliness. "Getting settled in, are you?"

"Yes, thanks."

"Getting a bit of a runaround from your form, I see." Evidently Maugham's quick-glancing dark eyes were observant. He went on without waiting for Cosmo to answer. "Don't worry, it always happens at first. I can remember going through it too. The main thing is to keep calm about it, don't go howling to old Gabby. That doesn't help, it only puts people's backs up."

"Yes, that's what I thought."

"Good lad. Actually—here's something else to cheer you up—the brighter you are, the worse you get it. Nobody bothers to give hell to boringly dull stick-in-the-muds."

"I hadn't thought of that," Cosmo said.

"I expect you are quite bright, aren't you? Isn't your father in research, and Professor Doom your aunt or cousin or something? My father says she has a theory that space comes round in a circle and overlaps with itself and she's bound to get the Nobel Prize one of these years.—Hey, would you like to be in a play, young Curtis? I'm going to put one on next term—All Aboard the Wooden Horse, or, Tales of the Trojan War. Lots of sword-fighting. You like acting?"

"Yes, very much." He and Mark and Ma had improvised dozens of plays.

"Okay, that's a date then." Maugham went whistling round the corner to the Senior common-room. Cosmo climbed the coconut-matted stairs and noticed brown-ringletted Tansy just ahead of him. She had obviously caught some of his conversation with Maugham.

"Just fancy!" she addressed the Remove form-room at large. "Our esteemed headboy says Dracula's Aunt is in line for the Nobel Prize. How about that, then? If that happens, there'll be no holding our Wonder Boy. He'll *really* be too big for his boots."

"Well, old Maugham ought to know," Chris said. "His dad's a physicist at Nuffield. Mannering Professor of Astro-Physics."

"I am surprised that *you* know what the Nobel Prize *is*, Tansy dear," Moley drawled gently.

Cosmo suddenly realized something he felt he had been a fool not to notice earlier—Moley did not like the silly spiteful Tansy in the least. In fact, gradually, the form's flat façade of hostility was beginning to break up under his quiet scrutiny of it; now he could distinguish the different people, see the light and shade around them. Tansy, for instance, at age six—he'd be ready to bet she'd have been just like horrible little Con, jumping up and down, bawling, "Tansy come too, Tansy come too!" He chuckled a little at the thought, and caught a quick glance from Moley—not exactly friendly, but not unfriendly either—a measuring, interested glance.

Mr Cheevy shot into the room. "Why isn't everybody sitting down, may I ask? And why do I only see five books on the desk in front of me?—Ah, about time, too—" as six more people hastily handed in their homework. "Right, now today we are to consider circles. Tansy, how do you suppose that circles differ from triangles?"

"They're round, sir," Tansy said, giggling.

"*Round.*" Mr Cheevy's small, red-rimmed eyes rested on Tansy with dislike. "Can anybody expand on that somewhat self-evident answer? You, Cosmo."

"Well, sir: triangles are all different from each other. But circles are all the same. You could put them all inside each other and they'd fit."

Mr Cheevy's eyebrows shot up. "We are to go all over the world collecting circles and stacking them inside each other? Like hoop-la hoops?"

Everybody giggled sycophantically. Mr Cheevy scowled.

"Well—as it happens—Cosmo is perfectly right. You

could stack the circles. You couldn't stack triangles. Now, let us get down to basics ... "

On Friday Cosmo saw the Rolls arrive with slightly mixed feelings. Would he have been happier to stay at school? It wasn't that members of his form were condescending to speak to him yet – or, at least, if they did, it was only in derisive questions:

"Well, Cosmic, how are your three dear pals at home? Percy, Bert, and charming Oscar? Did they enjoy their Mars bars? And has Dracula's Aunt been robbing any tombs lately?"

"You can't wonder that Cosmic knows all about the difference between circles and triangles. Dracula's Aunt probably keeps him busy all weekend proving Pythagoras while she gets on with her knitting. 'Oh, Cosmic dear, just come here and hold the square on the hypotenuse while I cast off, will you, there's a good little chappie.'"

He was wearily used to such tedious stuff by now and able to endure it with calm. However: it was not that he would actually *prefer* to stay at school over the weekend – but he couldn't help wondering about the big fair-haired boy – Con. Whether he would put in an appearance. How large he would be if so. What he would be doing.

If Eunice had phoned to say that she and Mrs Tydings were going off to Brighton for the weekend and he must stay in Oxford, he would not have been exactly appalled. But she did not.

After lunch on Friday Cosmo went to Miss Gracie at the store and bought three bars of plain nut chocolate. "For your friends again?" she said smiling at him.

"Yes," he said.

"For dear Percy, dear Bertie, and dear Ossie," murmured Charley, behind him in the queue.

"I've never noticed *you* buying chocolate for your friends," Miss Gracie rather tartly remarked, and Charley looked a little abashed.

Cosmo put the chocolate in his duffel-bag and was ready for Eunice when she arrived.

She gave a gracious bow to the reception committee that called "Goodbye, Dracula's Aunt!" as they left.

"I'm going to drop you at home," she said when they were out of Oxford, "and get changed and then drive back into town. I have to dine in Hall tonight because a distinguished Viennese mathematician is visiting the college. You won't mind my not being there, will you? I'll be back by midnight and Emma is just across the way – or you can sleep in her house if you feel at all nervous."

"No, no, I'll be quite all right," Cosmo assured her. None the less he did feel a slight sinking as Eunice, having put on a long white dress and some silver jewellery, took off again.

"Ain't she smashing with her hair done so posh," said Mrs Tydings fondly, and Cosmo noticed that Eunice had her hair drawn up in a great silver-yellow sweep and looked quite like a model or a film actress – not in the least like a possible Nobel Prize winner.

"See you later!" she called and waved.

"I'll come too to open the gates," Cosmo shouted on a sudden impulse, and sprinted and jumped on to the running-board of the Rolls. "I can walk back. Then you won't get your dress dusty."

Strolling slowly back along the farm track he wondered if he was a coward. And, if so, whether a coward was such a shameful thing to be. Was it possible *not* to be afraid?

There was the mill house, rosy and smiling among its dark trees, in the last rays of the sun. What might be inside it, or lurking near by?

It still lacked an hour to supper-time ("Cheese pudding," Mrs Tydings told him. "I always have that when Miss Eunice goes out, because she don't like cheese pudding.") Cosmo decided to make a start on his platform in the walnut tree. First he had to construct a rope pulley to raise his planks from the ground. And then he had to measure the length of the planks that he would need.

The work went ahead steadily. Four planks were cut to the right length, hauled up, and nailed into place, supported by chocks of wood. About two more—maybe three—would finish that part of the job. Then he'd have to fix a guard-rail round his platform—he thought he had better consult Mr Marvell about that. He had a notion that smallish logs or posts would be better than planks; a guard-rail ought to be fairly strong. But if he used posts he would need extra-long nails to hold them in place.

Looking down the trunk at this point he started, and nearly dropped his hammer. For the fair-haired boy was standing down below, gazing up at him, hands on hips, with a measuring, frowning stare.

"What are you doing there?" Cosmo called. "What do you want?"

The boy didn't answer.

Mrs Tydings came to the kitchen door.

"Cosmo? Are you up there? The cheese pudding will be ready in five minutes exactly! So just you come down now and wash your hands. If there's one thing I can't abide, it's to see a cheese pudding spoil because somebody's late."

"Okay, okay, I'm coming!"

When Cosmo reached the foot of the tree the boy had

gone. So, Cosmo later discovered, had the three chocolate bars out of his duffel-bag.

He went to bed in a very thoughtful frame of mind.

He hadn't been asleep more than half an hour when he was abruptly woken by somebody shaking him hard.

"Wake up! Wake up, lazybones! And hurry up about it!"

"What's the big rush? What's going on? Is there a fire?" Startled out of his first heavy sleep, Cosmo was not fully awake yet; he was back in Australia, where bush-fires had always been their great fear; he thought it was Mark waking him.

But it was the fair-haired boy.

A slip of moon shone in at the window so that the room was not wholly dark. Cosmo saw the light shine on the boy's eyes, and on something he wore round his neck; it gleamed as Eunice's silver necklace had done.

"What do you want?" Cosmo demanded again. He was very much afraid, but tried not to show it. Until now, he had encouraged himself with the thought that, although the boy could be seen – at least by Cosmo and perhaps by Lob – he was not really solid, but just dangled in the air like a mirage or a rainbow. There had been no question, though, as to the solidity of those thin muscular hands that had pulled him out of bed.

"Put on your clothes. Hurry!"

"Why should I? First you steal my chocolate and then you wake me – I don't know who you think you are – "

"I am Con," the fair boy said simply.

"*Was* that you, last week, then? Why are you so much bigger this week? Or are there two Cons?"

"I don't understand."

"Why did you take my sweets?"

82

"The sweet food? Because if I eat something that is yours, then we are part of one another, and you must help me. Also it makes me strong."

Cosmo did not fancy the sound of this, but at least it must mean that Con was not precisely hostile to him—not if he needed help—though he did not seem friendly, either; he stood watching with an impatient expression as Cosmo pulled on jeans and sweater.

"Why do I have to get up in the middle of the ruddy night?"

"Because I have very little time. *You* can do as you please all day," Con said, looking at him with what now seemed angry scorn. "You can play or learn from books or amuse yourself, but I have to work. I am a slave, I must do as my master tells me."

"A *slave?*"

"What do you think this is?" Con touched the ring round his neck. Cosmo saw that it was a metal collar, fastened with a lock.

"But why are you a slave?"

They were now slipping quietly down the shallow polished stairs. Mrs Tydings had gone to her own house long ago. They crossed the brick-floored main room to the outer door. Lob, by the glowing ash-heap which was all that was left of the fire, rumbled a growl in his throat, but, when he saw Cosmo, stayed lying down.

Cosmo softly opened the door and they went out on to the dewy lawn.

"I am a slave because, though my father was a free Roman soldier, my mother is a Silurian slave-woman from Maridu-num," Con said sourly.

"Is she still alive?" Cosmo asked with a pang of envy.

"Yes, but her master is a magistrate and he has gone south to Isca, and I was sold to the Prefect here."

"What work do you have to do?"

"Clean his house. Look after his horses and his hounds. And now I have to fight."

"Fight? What kind of fighting?"

"This kind," said Con.

He picked up a three-pronged trident which lay at the foot of the walnut tree. "I am to be a net-and-trident man. I fight against swordsmen. My master will be betting on me, so I have to fight well."

"You're a gladiator?"

"Yes, yes!" Con said impatiently. "A retiarius. I am to fight in the Games at Corinium. But first I have to practise. You are to help me. Come, hurry, fight, fight!"

"Why should I?"

"You are to *help* me!" Con said again furiously. "Fight, man! Where is your sword?"

"I haven't *got* a sword."

"*You have no sword?* Although you are free?" Con seemed terribly taken aback at this piece of information; also filled with unspeakable scorn. Cosmo began to feel that the other boy thought him a very poor sort of creature—perhaps he was?

"*I* could use the net, and *you* could use the trident?" he suggested diffidently. "Or the other way round? I believe they did it like that sometimes?"

Con looked doubtful.

"Is it so very urgent?"

"Of course it is urgent. Seven days from now is the day of the Games. Very well—if you truly have no sword—that is what we shall have to do. You may have the trident first."

84

The trident was unexpectedly heavy—like a big, deadly toasting-fork with sharpened steel points that could probably do horrible damage if stabbed into a vital spot. Cosmo found it quite hard to wield—his arms were still pretty stiff from hammering—also he did not want to hurt the other boy. Con had no such scruples. As they feinted and sparred and zigzagged across the lawn, Cosmo realized that, even if Con had not had much chance to practise this kind of fighting, still at least he must have watched a good many bouts; he used the net with a deadly sort of skill in dozens of different ways, whirling it, sometimes, spread open in the air above Cosmo, who had to duck and plunge to avoid it; sometimes swishing it, bunched together into a rope, along the ground, in a bid to knock his opponent's feet from under him, so that Cosmo had to bound high to escape it. Well, at least, those boring games of Dodge-ball were useful for *something*, he thought dispassionately, leaping, then ducking, and somewhere in between the two movements managing to work in a lunge at the other boy's ribs. The net was heavier and slower to wield; Cosmo's advantage must obviously lie in nimbleness and dexterity, in making dozens of swift little feints and stabs; however, in spite of this planned intention he found that most of the time Con kept him on the defensive, whirling the net confusingly round Cosmo's head like a matador's cape, driving him back and back until he was up against the cartshed wall. At last by a cunning double swooping motion—down, then up in a fish-shaped curve—Con managed to entangle Cosmo completely, and brought him to the ground with a thud.

"Habet!" he panted. "One to me! Now we change weapons."

At first Cosmo found the net wholly unmanageable. It was just a clumsy, loose, heavy, bulky bundle of material—

85

how in the world could it be turned into a killing weapon? Who ever first had the stupid notion of fighting with a net, anyway? Twice Con jabbed him with the trident—before, suddenly enraged, he discovered the knack of sending the mesh whistling through the air like a cowboy's rope. But Con—perhaps from his work of looking after horses—seemed absolutely tireless, unbelievably active and light on his feet, pivoting and bounding in and out. It was the despair of sheer exhaustion in the end—heaven only knew how long they had been fighting, but it seemed like the whole night—that gave Cosmo the idea for a feint with the net, shooting out one corner of it in a lightning-quick flip to catch his opponent's eye on his right side, while keeping the main breadth of the fabric bundled into his own right hand, ready to fling out and drop as Con turned—"*Got you!*" he gasped exultantly, as the heavy mass fell envelopingly over the fair tousled head.

"That was a good trick you used," Con said with approval as he scrambled up from his knees. "I will remember that at the Games ... Who taught it you?"

"Nobody. I just made it up."

Con looked at him wide-eyed. "Made it up? And yet you spend your life in idle play—"

"Hey—here comes my cousin." Cosmo had seen the glimmering headlights of the Rolls, boring their way down through the dark shoulder of the wood. "We shall have to stop."

"I am tired, in any case," Con said simply. "We shall fight again tomorrow."

He gathered up his net and turned, seeming to slither off sideways into a vertical crack in space.

"Good heavens, Cosmo," said Eunice, stepping out of the car. "You haven't been up all this time?"

"No, I did go to bed ... But then I got up and came out again. Did you have a good time with your Viennese professor?"

"No! He was a thundering old bore," Eunice said cheerfully, shutting the heavy front door behind her. "His mind fossilized back in the 1920s." She gave a great yawn. "Goodnight, Cosmo. See you in the morning."

When Cosmo fell into bed for the second time that night he was physically tired – absolutely bushed, in fact – but his mind was in a tingle of wakefulness. First, the fighting had been terrific – fast, skilled, exhilarating – he had no idea that a combat of that kind could be made into such a stylish, sparkling affair. Now that he had time to think about it, he had several more good ideas for feints with both net and trident – why didn't they do that at school instead of those terrible games with bean-bags? He was really looking forward to more practice with Con, towards whom his whole attitude had completely changed. Sure, Con was a bit surly and aggressive, but if you were born a slave and the child of a slave, what could anybody expect? "Will you always be a slave?" Cosmo had asked at one point, jabbing with the trident. "No," Con panted, flipping the net expertly first to the left, then to the right – "Sometimes – if you fight well – and the crowd like you – the Governor may give you your freedom as a reward. But you're more likely to get killed, of course," he added, matter-of-factly.

At another point – when Con had netted him and he was carefully freeing himself from the entangling folds – Cosmo had asked,

"Do you remember helping me and my, brother once damming a brook, long ago?"

"I don't know what you mean," Con had answered.

It was no use asking him that kind of question, Cosmo

87

concluded; his mind didn't seem to retain events that were out of his own scheme of time.

But a very decent fellow on his own terms. Worth a dozen of Chris or Lot or Andy or Charley ... Cosmo fell asleep.

Next day Cosmo was rather startled, coming downstairs, to discover Con stretched out asleep in a patch of sunlight on the brick floor, in the angle of the wall under the window. Lob knew he was there all right, he growled mutteringly from time to time as he chewed and worried at little bits of dirt and thorns between his toes, causing Eunice to look up from her coffee and newspaper to say, "What's up, Lobby boy? Rheumatics bothering you today?"

Neither she nor Mrs Tydings could see Con. It was really peculiar; you'd think they'd be able to hear his slow, deep breathing and occasional sighs as he shifted position.

After breakfast Cosmo went and helped Mr Marvell with jobs around the farm. Presently he asked advice about the guard-rail. "I should think what would be best for you," said Mr Marvell after reflecting, "would be a two-three fence bars, split down the middle. You won't want 'em too heavy, or they'll be a nuisance to get up and a nuisance to fix; but, as you say, you do want 'em solid enough to do their job. I know where there's just the thing for you; Look–" and he showed Cosmo a stack of weathering ash poles about four inches in diameter. "Those'll do you nicely; when all the work's done, 's evening, I'll help you split as many as you're likely to need. That's an awkward job, no joke to do on your own."

After thanking Mr Marvell, Cosmo decided to tackle his homework next; a thin drizzle had begun to fall, it seemed a good time to get school work out of the way. But later on the weather began to clear, and a watery sun shone out; Cosmo was able to raise his last two planks and fix them into place. Then, looking down, he saw Con climbing up the pitons.

"This is a good lookout spot you have made," the other boy said, reaching Cosmo's platform. "You would be safe from wolves – or even from armed men, if you had weapons."

He surveyed the platform with critical approval. It now covered an area of roughly sixteen square feet, but had a very asymmetrical shape, governed by the splay of the big walnut branches; *Irregular*, Cosmo thought with a private grin, thinking of Flatland: "If a man with a triangular front and a polygonal back were allowed to propagate a still more Irregular posterity, what would become of the arts of life?"

He wished he could talk to Con about Flatland.

Instead he explained about the need for guard-rails.

"I will help you split them," Con said at once. "And then we can fight up here; this would be a fine place to practise."

"*Fight up here?*"

"It would make us more nimble and more careful," Con said.

Cosmo didn't care for the idea at all, but he could hardly refuse Con's offer of help. The two of them climbed down and went round to the back of the big Dutch haybarn, where the poles were stacked, in the angle of that and another building that had once been a dairy. Mr Marvell had shown Cosmo where to find an axe, a mallet, and some wedges. Splitting, as Mr Marvell had said, was an awkward job; even with the two of them it went slowly, accompanied by some curses.

"One cannot be a retiaruis without fingers," Con said, snatching his hand away just in time on one occasion.

"I don't know *what* you could be without fingers."

"A scribe, and use the other hand. Or a clerk, and work on an abacus."

It was true, Cosmo reflected, that you did not need fingers for mathematics; but he was more careful after that, and by dusk they had half a dozen poles split and hoisted up on to the platform.

"Tomorrow we fasten them in place," Con said. "Tonight we fight on the grass again."

Cosmo did wonder how Eunice would react to the sight of him apparently fighting nobody – if she should happen to look out; but there was a television programme about bible history which both she and Mrs Tydings wanted to watch. No objections were raised to his going out in the dark, provided he stayed away from the weir.

"But tomorrow night you must be in early, as it's school next day."

School for me, he thought, and the Games for Con; which would I choose if I had the choice?

Fighting that night went better; went very well indeed.

"You are a terrific fighter, Con," he said.

"And you are none so bad yourself."

"Surely you'll win all your fights and be given your freedom?"

"Ah," said Con gloomily, "that depends on many things. They free only a few men at each Games; there may be others, swordsmen or sling-men, who are better than I. And they have very fine fighters at Corinium – the best men from all over the country, even from Gaul. No, I try not to hope for freedom. Hope is a bad friend; it can make your arm shake and your eye uncertain. It is best to keep one's mind clear of hope. I just work to be a good fighter. After all, fighting is what we are here for, isn't it? Besides – " he paused, frowning down at the trident which he held, jabbing it into the grass.

"Besides what, Con?"

"There is a prophecy concerning my family," Con said uncertainly.

Cosmo felt as if a cold finger had been drawn across his midriff.

"A prophecy?"

"I had it from my mother; she, from my father. The eldest son always dies young, dies fighting ... I am my father's firstborn."

"Oh, but – That isn't – Con, look here, you don't *have* to believe that you are going to die – "

"No?" Con said, but he said it without conviction. "Come, let us fight again."

Mr Marvell had been very surprised to find that all the fence poles had been split without his help.

"Well, you are a worker," he said. "I can see you'll be a big help come haymaking and harvest time." Cosmo felt something of a fraud. "Now you'll want some four-inch nails for them, and a bit of wire as well, if you take my advice; you want them guard-rails really firm. Nail them first, with the nails a bit countersunk, then truss 'em to the boughs with a good splicing of wire. Or that's what *I'd* do if it were me."

Cosmo thought this very good advice. The job of attaching the guard-rails proved unexpectedly long and fiddling; the rails had to be tapered and notched to fit the branches that they met; doing this and fixing them in position took most of the day, interspersed with a few jobs for Eunice in the garden.

"Now we fight," said Con, at sunset.

The light was already thickening. By now, Cosmo felt even less keen about fighting up on the platform, so many feet above the ground, even with the guard-rails.

"Well; okay," he said half-heartedly. "But only a couple of bouts – I vote we stop when it gets dark. Which do you want first – net or trident?"

"I will take the net," said Con. He picked it up, shook it expertly into folds, and slung it over his arm. "Are you ready? On guard, then!"

But as Cosmo began to move cautiously across the platform with the trident, feinting a little this way and that, Con turned his head suddenly, alertly, listening.

"Stop a moment!"

"What is it?"

"I hear my master calling. Curse it – I must go. Quick, give me the trident." He took it from Cosmo and dropped it to the ground, where it stuck quivering. Con made for the entrance to the platform, then turned to say, "You have been a good friend to me. I thank you for that."

His bony right hand clasped that of Cosmo for a moment; he almost smiled; then seemed to glide into a crack of air, like a lizard between two bricks, and was gone.

For a moment Cosmo could hardly believe that he was alone. Con's presence had been so real to him. He felt almost suffocated with mixed feelings, and among them regret was the foremost. Something about that handclasp had filled him with a certainty that he would not be seeing Con again.

"Cosmo?" called Eunice down below. "Are you still up in your eyrie? Don't you think you had better be coming down before it is pitch dark?"

"Yes, I'm just coming," he answered, and clambered carefully down the pitons.

"I must say, it is a remarkably successful project," she said, waiting for him down below. "Mr Marvell is greatly impressed. Don't you think you ought to invite somebody from school just to get the benefit of it?"

"Oh no – not just yet," Cosmo said quickly.

He tried to imagine showing it to one of his enemies from Remove, Charley or Chris. They would probably think that Mr Marvell had done it all. Pampered little namby-pamby Cosmo. Or one of the girls, Tansy or Sheil. They would want to have a dolls' tea-party up there.

"Not just yet," he repeated.

"Well, you know best," Eunice said comfortably. "Friends come in their own time."

5

Bun and Meredith

IT SEEMED HARDLY POSSIBLE to Cosmo that he was beginning on his fourth week of school. Only one more to go and then it would be the Easter holidays – wonderful thought! Four whole weeks of days spent doing what he chose at the mill, or working with Mr Marvell, who had all kinds of activities planned – helping to break the young horses, Punch and Juno, and accustom them to harness, learning to plough, going to fetch some black-spotted lambs from Witney who would be about ready to leave their mothers by then, building a new pig-pen ... And Eunice had some plans too; she had suggested badger-watching in the wood one night – fishing – mending the two leaky boats that were drawn up in a boathouse on the island, turning the cartshed into an indoor tennis-court and playing Henry V's kind of tennis there. And he still had not explored the mill buildings ...

With all that to look forward to, and Con to think back over, it did seem as if the week at school should be bearable enough. But where was Con now?

Did Con cease to exist when he slid back into his own

dimension – as far as Cosmo was concerned? Or do I cease to exist for him? Cosmo wondered, getting out of the Rolls and waving goodbye to Eunice. Mr Falaise, who taught maths to the upper forms, and Latin to Remove, happened to be on the front steps at that moment. It seemed that he and Eunice had been to college together, and he said to her a little wistfully,

"I don't suppose you'd have time to come and talk to the Seniors one day, about relativity or something, would you? It would be such a nice change for them from all that dull stuff they have to do with me!"

"I'll see, Benny," Eunice said laughing. "I'm awfully busy at the moment – writing my book you know – but I'll come along sometime, I promise."

She had told Cosmo a little about her book. "It's a kind of mathematical judo. Wriggling about, coming out in unexpected places. Trying to get the best result with the least effort."

"What are you going to call it?"

"Not quite sure yet. *Man and Measurement*, perhaps. After all, when you think about it, man is the only animal who has taken to measuring. In fact, that seems to be one of the things we were mainly designed for – legs, arms and feet for measuring, toes and fingers for counting, minds for calculating – if we'd been whales, how differently we'd have turned out!"

Cosmo went in to school thinking about this.

If man was so good at measuring, why did he have to fight, too? Con had said he was here to fight. Measuring and fighting seemed highly contradictory pursuits. Or were there, perhaps, two sorts of people, the measuring kind, and the fighting kind?

"And how's our dear Wonder Boy today?" said Tansy.

Cosmo ignored her; and it seemed to him that several others in the form were also beginning to find that joke a trifle stale.

Glancing around as he dropped his homework books on the staff table, he noticed that something seemed to be amiss with Meredith. Usually he found her face rather satisfying despite its bleak expression—it was such a clear, shapely oval, with large eyes of a strange, very beautiful greenish-grey, fringed by black lashes. Her face was his favourite among those of the girls, if you can have a favourite among enemies. But today it was swollen and blurred, its pallor blotchy, the whites of her eyes reddened.

"What's up with Meredith?" he murmured to Bun, as they crossed the garden to prayers in the school hall. As he had reckoned, stupid Bun was not going to place obedience to form rule above the passing on of a noteworthy piece of news.

"Her mother died," he whispered. Charley kicked him sharply on the shin, and he quickly shuffled to a place farther away from Cosmo, who felt a sharp twinge of sympathy for Meredith. Poor wretch—perhaps that was why she had been called to Gabby's office last week—to be told that her mother was ill. And now she had died—and while Meredith was away from home, too. He wondered if she would go home for the funeral. And then thought of his father's latest letter.

"We had a memorial service for your mother and Mark, since it is not possible to have a funeral for people who are only presumed dead. But *something* seemed needed—to say that their lives had been of value, to round them off."

Glancing to his right—as usual, he had taken the place at the end of the row, so that only one of his form-mates would be able to demonstrate disgust at having to stand next to him – Cosmo saw that the person next to him was Meredith. Evidently she was too sunk in grief to care where she stood. During prayers he noticed her surreptitiously dab at her eyes a couple of times with a tissue. Going out afterwards he ventured, taking advantage of the general bustle and shuffle, to murmur in her ear,

"I'm awfully sorry about your mother, Meredith."

She glanced back at him in surprise, and he noticed that, though the whites of her eyes were reddened, the dark green–grey of the pupils was still beautiful – like moss on a grey rock. She did not reply, but made a tiny movement of her head, a faint acknowledgment. This encouraged him to add,

"I know what it's like. Mine died two months ago."

At that she looked round at him full and clear, eyes opened wide. To his hurt astonishment there was now blazing scorn in her face. She said,

"I don't believe you! And I call it pretty cheap to invent a thing like *that*, just to get attention."

Then she took two hasty steps, so as to catch up with Sheil, and grabbed her arm.

Cosmo felt as if he had been slapped. His cheeks stung with rage and hurt. He would let himself be fried in boiling oil before he offered any sympathy to *her* again. Blast her! He was enraged at having laid himself open to her retort by his stupid, spongy craving for sympathy. Con wouldn't have done such a thing. Con would probably let his skin be peeled off inch by inch before he expected *anybody* to offer sympathy for anything – and, from now on, Cosmo would be the same. Hunching his shoulders, he followed the rest of his form in to lessons.

The black mood that followed this incident lay on Cosmo for several days; he did not care whether anybody in Remove spoke to him or not. In fact he preferred his own thoughts. He had plenty of *them*.

Sliding in the playroom after supper with Frances and Tim had begun to seem decidedly boring and babyish, and he now spent most of his evenings in the library, reading. He had discovered, with great pleasure, sequels of several books that he and Mark had owned (the ones that were following across the sea in a box; heaven only knew when they would arrive); he had read *Jan, Son of Finn, The Second Jungle Book*, and *The Box of Delights*. But on Thursday night when he went up to the library he found to his great frustration that a staff meeting was about to begin there, and he was not allowed in.

"Well, you can change your book if you are quick, Cosmo," Miss Nivven told him kindly, "and then go and read it in your own form-room."

All in a hurry Cosmo grabbed *Kim*, which he had read several times, and turned to leave. Read in his own form-room indeed! Ha, what a hope! But then he thought, Well, why shouldn't I go in there if I want to? I've a perfect right to read in there if I choose. Con would think I was crazy if I didn't, and he strolled in, trying to look unconcerned.

Two things struck him instantly – that there was a rather hectic, feverish, giggly atmosphere in the room, and that, for once, it was not aimed at or concentrated on him.

In fact, apart from a couple of chilly stares, he was ignored. He slipped into his seat, pulled out pad and pencil, and started writing a letter to Con.

"Dear Con," he wrote, "I wonder what you would make of the people at this school. I think you might find them pretty childish ... "

The people in the room – there were eight of them, everybody, in fact, but the two day-boys – seemed to be engaged in talking about snuff. Listening to them, as he invented his imaginary letter, Cosmo wondered what there was in snuff to make them all so excited and conspiratorial.

"*My* father always uses rappee," said Moley learnedly. "He prefers to buy a coarse snuff and then re-grind it himself, flavouring it in the process with bergamot oil and coriander bark. But I prefer a lighter snuff myself."

"Do *you* take snuff, Moley?" Bun asked wonderingly.

"But of course. Always, in the holidays. Don't you?"

"No," said Bun.

"You *don't take snuff*, Bun?" exclaimed Tansy, giggling. "Well you are a stick-in-the-mud! *Everybody* else does. What sort do you take, Charley?"

"Oh, I usually prefer a dry snuff," drawled Charley. "I use a Welsh mixture mostly – that's roasted before it is ground, you know."

"*I* like a moist, spiced snuff," put in Sheil. "And I like it scented with cloves and attar of roses. Remind me to show you my snuff-box, some time, Bun; it's a very pretty one; I keep it upstairs in my work-basket."

It now became plain to Cosmo that an elaborate tease of Bun was in process; evidently his classmates had temporarily lost interest in Cosmo as a target and were using their waspish energy in other directions.

"You really *ought* to take snuff, you know, Bun," Chris said. "It's pretty childish not to. I daresay even our Wonder Boy along there would admit to taking snuff if anyone were to ask him."

Cosmo felt this was some kind of challenge. Was he going to buy acceptance at the price of baiting Bun? He decided not to be drawn in.

Bun became very flustered and apologetic. "But I don't know how to take snuff! Or where to get it! Where do I

99

go? Can I get it from a shop? No one has ever told me about snuff before."

"Oh, you needn't worry about that," Charley reassured him kindly. "Well, you *can* get it from tobacconists, of course, but until you have actually decided which kind you prefer, it's much better to go to Mr Gabbitas and ask his advice."

Here many nudges and significant looks were exchanged; it became plain to Cosmo where the course of the tease was leading.

"I couldn't do *that*!" exclaimed Bun, alarmed. "Ask Mr Gabbitas? I *couldn't*!"

"But don't you see, that's what he's there for. To advise you. Just you go and knock on his door — he's in his office now, I happen to know, having coffee — and you say to him, 'I'd like to try a little of your snuff, Mr Gabbitas, please.'"

"Oh, no, I couldn't do that," protested poor Bun, but it was plain that, none thel ess, he was fascinated by the idea, almost hypnotized by it.

"You really should, you know," Rebecca soberly assured him. "Just think how we shall all feel when we are in first Intermediate, and you still aren't taking snuff."

Everybody endorsed this.

"We shall feel *ashamed* of you, Bun. When we're all in studies and you not knowing about snuff."

"You might have to stop down in Remove for another year."

"Oh my goodness," said Bun, moithered and distracted. "Might I? I shouldn't like that. Oh, all right then, I'll go. But tell me again what I have to say."

Cosmo noticed that among all the teasing chorus, Meredith was the only one who had not spoken. She was sitting silent, with her chin on her hands, wrapped in her own thoughts.

"Even Cosmo here will tell you that you ought to go to Mr Gabbitas, Bun," said Charley, giving Cosmo a measuring look. "Won't you, Wonder Boy? And I'm sure Dracula's Aunt would agree, too. I'm sure *she* takes snuff."

"Should I go to Mr Gabbitas, Cosmo?"

"No, Bun, don't be so silly. Can't you see they're pulling your leg?"

"Oh-oh," muttered Moley, "Cosmic doesn't approve of snuff for the young."

"I think you're all pretty childish if you want to know," Cosmo said. "Bun, they're making you go to Mr Gabbitas for a joke, can't you see?"

Despite this, Bun was at length persuaded to go to Mr Gabbitas; his classmates waited in delighted apprehension, seething with suppressed laughter, for the explosion.

Bun came back in a minute looking puzzled and quenched.

"He didn't do at all what you said he would; he just seemed cross! He had two ladies having coffee with him and he said, 'Don't be silly, Bunthorne, go away and don't bother me.'"

"Oh, you must have asked him in the wrong way,"said Charley, dying of laughter. "What did you say to him?"

"What you told me: 'Can I have some snuff, please, Mr Gabbitas.'"

"No, no, *no*, you should have said, 'I'd like to try a little snuff, Mr Gabbitas, *from your store*!' Now just you go back and have another try, using those words, and it'll work like a charm, you'll see."

Bun, red-faced and protesting, was urged to the door again.

"Oh, you are a lot of lunk-heads,' said Cosmo crossly

standing up. It was half-past eight, thank goodness, he could go to bed. "Why you get such a kick out of fooling that poor dummy, heaven only knows; I should have thought you could find something more interesting to do."

"Goody-goody-*gum-drop*," said Tansy into the startled silence that followed his words. Cosmo walked out and shut the door sharply behind him.

He went up to bed in a sad, angry, rebellious frame of mind.

He was thinking about his imaginary letter to Con.

I'd like to post it, he thought, but I can't. There's no way I can get in touch with Con. Or with Mark and Ma. They are lost to me, but why? I can write a letter to Father, put it in an envelope, stick a stamp on it, put it in the wooden box on the hall table, and somehow or other, from that box, it will find its way to Australia, eight thousand miles away. What proof have I that it will go from the box to Australia? None. Yet it does. Why isn't there some way of getting in touch with Con and Mark and Ma? That doesn't seem any more unlikely. I don't care a rap about laser beams or putting men on Mars—why can't scientists work harder on getting in touch with people who have gone?

He wrote in his diary, "Everyone in Remove teasing poor Bun", and went to sleep. At once he started dreaming about Mark, who, oddly, was wearing glasses, which he had not in real life. He was deep in some book, and very exasperated because Cosmo wanted to talk to him—as Mark often had been. He couldn't stand being bothered when he was reading—that was the one thing that shook his equable temper.

"Do go away, Cosmo," he said in the dream. "Don't bother me now. You can look at my butterflies if you want."

Mark's butterflies! Cosmo half woke, moved by the

intensity of wondering what had happened to them. They had been a dazzling collection, not only Australian, but many from New Guinea, China, Japan. Mark had bought and collected and corresponded and swapped with immense diligence and had them all beautifully housed in three Japanese lacquer cabinets. What would become of them? Father could hardly bring them to England. At one time it had been the height of Cosmo's ambition to possess the beautiful things – Mark had only rarely allowed him to look at them, because he said being exposed to light too often would fade their colours. But since Mark's death somehow the thought of owning them had lost its appeal for Cosmo. Probably Father would give them to a museum ...

Next day, just as the members of Remove were about to go and wash their hands for lunch, Mr Gabbitas swept into the room in a cold rage. Cosmo had only seen the headmaster in benign moods before, and was interested to find that he *could* be in a rage – he had appeared to be such a mild, milk-and-watery man. Now he was quite white with anger, so that, with his thinness, pale eyes, white hair, brows, and lashes, and his quick, whipping movements, he looked like a white-coated ferret, or perhaps, Cosmo thought, some thin, dry, white, venomous furry snake, angry and dangerous. Bun had already left the room, summoned by Mrs Robinson to be measured for a new blazer. Old Gabby looked sharply round the form-room.

"Priest and Salford can go to lunch," he said. Andy and Lot left. "I've something to say to the rest of you," Mr Gabbitas went on. "Last night you all conspired together in a particularly stupid, childish, and spiteful manner to make a fool of poor Bunthorne. And also of me. *I* can look after myself – though I intensely dislike being bothered by silly practical jokes at the end of a hard day, and when I have visitors – but poor Bunthorne, as you are perfectly well aware, is not capable of understanding such jokes. You hurt, upset, and bothered him. I hope you are all thoroughly ashamed of yourselves."

Nobody spoke. He stared at the row of downcast, unresponsive faces, and went on,

"Your punishment for this piece of childishness is that nobody will be allowed to go out or home during the weekend. You can stay in and do extra Latin prep, which Mr Falaise will set you. And I hope that will persuade you to behave less irresponsibly in future."

He turned to leave amid a collective gasp. Really that was going it a bit strong! But no one had the courage to protest.

Meredith, however, put up her hand.

"Yes, Meredith, what is it?" Mr Gabbitas modified his tone slightly when addressing her, but then made matters worse by adding, "I must say, I am very surprised at *you*, Meredith, getting involved in such a mean joke, specially just now. – Well, what is it?"

Meredith went scarlet, then pale again. Somebody was heard to mutter, "Unfair old bastard."

Collecting herself, Meredith said, "Sir, Cosmo Curtoys oughtn't to be punished. He didn't – didn't take part in the snuff joke. In fact he tried to persuade Bun not to go to you and – and said that we were a lot of lunk-heads."

"Oh, he did, did he?" Mr Gabbitas looked at Cosmo sharply. "Well, I am not going to remit your punishment, Cosmo. You may think that unfair. But if you were clear enough about the issue not to take part in the prank, you should have been able to dissuade them from it; or Bun from believing them. That is all I have to say. Now you may go down to lunch."

And he left the room.

Cosmo felt a deep sense of shock and outrage at the knowledge that he was prevented from going back to the mill house for another eight days. How was he going to bear it?

Then he realized that the rest of his classmates were looking at him commiseratingly.

"I must say that's a bit thick on you, Cosmo," Charley said.

"Jolly hard cheese," Chris remarked.

"Gabby really is a cunning old bounder," Moley murmured.

"Poor Wonder Boy gets the thin end of both wedges," Tansy giggled.

Sheil said, "Damn that man! Damn him! My sister was going to take me to the ballet."

"Thanks for sticking up for me, anyway," Cosmo said to Meredith.

"Oh, I daresay you would have stuck up for yourself if I hadn't," she replied coldly.

"Wouldn't have done any good, anyway," Chris said. "Oh well, now we're stuck with Cosmic for the weekend."

"Don't let it worry you. I shan't get in your hair," said Cosmo, and went downstairs to lunch, thinking how horrible and embarrassing it was going to be to have to tell Eunice, right there on the front steps, that he was not allowed to come home.

However, to his surprise, Mr Gabbitas stopped him on the stairs after lunch and told him that he had already telephoned Professor Doom and explained the situation. "And I may as well add, Cosmo, that I appreciate you must feel your punishment as—ah—somewhat unjust. But I fancied that if you were the *only* person to go unpunished it might—ah—exacerbate your difficulties with the rest of your form."

"I see, sir." Wily old character! Cosmo thought. Moley was right. He sees more than he gets given credit for. Maybe Maugham had said something to him.

"Perhaps," Mr Gabbitas went on, "you will be able, in the course of the weekend, to get on to—ah—closer, more congenial terms with some of your companions."

Cosmo rather doubted this.

The following week crawled at tortoise speed. Every day seemed to last forty-eight hours. Not having the weekend as a springboard to get him through from Monday to Friday made Cosmo realize how much he owed to Eunice and Mrs Tydings and Mr Marvell, and how badly he would miss the mill house, the walnut tree, the weir, the island, the meadow, if he were to be deprived of them again.

Another exasperation was that this had been the weekend of the full moon.

"Blast it!" he exclaimed, when he saw it sailing past the window on Saturday night.

"Now what?" said Chris, morosely doing Latin—Mr Falaise had co-operated by giving them an immense amount of translation.

Cosmo couldn't help noticing that his classmates had somewhat relaxed their ban, and begun speaking to him occasionally. He supposed he ought to be grateful for this. But he did not answer Chris; if he had explained that he was sore at missing a phantom coach-and-six, it would have sent him back to square one.

Now he would have to wait till the next full moon.

At last Friday came. It was the end of term. All the rest

of the boarders had gone off early, in a ferment of excitement, with large trunks stuffed full of their possessions and the things they had made in handwork. By lunchtime Cosmo had the Remove form-room to himself, since Eunice had her lecture in the morning as usual and could not pick him up earlier than on any other Friday. He did not mind. It felt peaceful in there, leaning on the sill, looking out into the Woodstock Road, watching the excited bustle of taxis arriving, listening to the slamming of car doors and shouted goodbyes. There was even a kind of security in knowing that they would all be coming back again next term. It was not like his goodbye to Con.

Somebody came into the room and he turned to see who it was.

"Oh, hullo," said Meredith. "Not gone yet?"

"My cousin can't get here till this afternoon. How about you?"

"Oh— " she bit her lip. "I'm going to stay with my aunt. F— my father thinks I'd better not be at home, as he goes to his office all day, and I'd be alone."

"You mean you've got to stay with your aunt all the holidays? Do you like her house?"

"No. I hate it. It's in Northampton— a horrible town. I shan't have anything to do. There's nothing in the house— no books, nothing. Just for the last week of the holidays Father's going to take some leave, so I can go home. Only *one week* in my *own home*."

She seemed dazed by ill-fortune.

"That's an awful shame," Cosmo said. He added impulsively, "Shall I write to you?"

She gave him a doubtful look. "Well ... all right. Thanks. And I'll write back— though heaven knows what there'll be to write *about* in Northampton." Then she went on,

107

nervously, but gathering courage, "I'm sorry I was foul to you about – about your mother. Old Gab told me that she'd died. I'm sorry I didn't believe you."

Cosmo was tempted to say, "We still don't *know* if she died or not." But he kept silent. After a while he said, "That's all right. I hope it isn't too bad at your aunt's. – Listen, I can hear Mrs Robinson calling you."

"So she is. My hateful aunt must have arrived. Goodbye, Cosmo. See you in May."

"See you in May."

He heard her running down the stairs.

6

Sim

NEARLY TWO WEEKS AWAY from the place had made Cosmo almost begin to doubt the existence of the mill house; he could hardly believe in his own luck at being back. Everything was just the same: the sigh of the weir, old Lob stalking stately to meet him, his spiral of pitons glinting round the grey trunk of the walnut tree, Mr Marvell's ducks chuntering happily where the brook joined the river, and the sound of Blossom's whinny, up above the shoulder of woodland.

Everything was the same, but spring had advanced a notch or two: there were more leaves on the trees, the mud by the brook's edge was beginning to dry into flakes, some grape hyacinths were spots of blue in Eunice's flowerbed, and a pair of swallows were shooting in and out of the cartshed like Concorde without the noise.

"It's the best place in the world," he said to Mrs Tydings.

"It is that. How your father had the heart to go so far and stay so long, at the bottom back-end of the earth, I'll never know."

"He was trying to get away. But it didn't do any good."

"Made it worse. If it's laid on you, you ain't going to get

away, not if you go and sit on the South Pole. You might as well make up your mind to *that*. Two things I can't abide, one's running away, the other's turning your back on a thing and letting on as it ain't so, when it's staring you in the face. – Well, you run along out, my lamb – " they were washing the breakfast dishes – "and don't you plague Miss Eunice, for she's all wound up in her book."

"Of course I shan't!"

He ran out, steering a wide course round the end of the house where Eunice had her study. She really *was* wound up in her book, for she was correcting galley-proofs like long thick extra-wide sheets of loo paper, getting into a fearful tangle as she added more and more ink balloons full of mathematical formulae so that the proofs began to look like a mixture of a wormcast and an Ogham inscription. Eunice had told Cosmo about Ogham: it seemed a very useful and beautifully simple writing system, twenty different combinations of straight lines meeting each other; what a pity it was no longer used.

The sun, now, was really hot, and, though he did miss Con to a surprising degree – Con had been wonderful for doing things with, much better than Mark – Cosmo was so full of plans that he hardly knew where to start. The boats – the foals – he *still* hadn't explored the mill building; then there was his camp on the island where already new nettles were sprouting and he must fetch a sickle from the toolshed and cut them down – there was a lot to do.

Mr Marvell could be heard clanking buckets in the barnyard, so Cosmo went to help him first. The pigs were coming next week, so the most urgent job was to get the pigsty wall built. Mr Marvell had condemned the old pigsties as too small and insanitary; he was knocking the four of them into one.

"The sow's due to farrow three weeks after she gets here, so this'll do while the piglets are small," he explained, bashing away with a sledge-hammer. "Then I plan to let them run in the orchard so as to clear the ground, because that's full of nettle and dock. Pigs are good for clearing so long as you don't let 'em stay too long. Then the ground gets pigsick."

Rebuilding the sty took most of the next five days, on and off, and as an exchange, Mr Marvell gave Cosmo help and advice with the boats. One of them, an old skiff, was not in too bad shape; a morning's work with sealing compound and a couple of new pieces of planking made it reasonably watertight.

"Now you give her a day to dry off and a day soaking in the water to take up," said Mr Marvell. "And then she'll float like a nutshell. But keep away from the weir."

The other boat, a punt, was in a much worse state of repair; they left it out, turned bottom-side-up, to dry out completely before trying to estimate how much would need to be done to it.

Boats and water were something that had been missing from the life in Australia—except for those visits to the coast—and now Cosmo felt he could not have enough of them. He could never cross the footbridge without stopping in the middle to watch the waterweeds waving their long filaments, the fish slipping past, and the diagonal patterns made by the current, while time flowed by, whole quarter-hours together, as fast as the water, and more silently. (But Eunice said that time did not move—or at least, not in the way people imagined. Physics had showed that different things went at different speeds, or could even move in reverse directions. It was all rather hard to grasp.)

On the third morning after the boat-repair job, when

Cosmo ran to see if the skiff, left moored under the foot-bridge, had taken much water during the night, he was indignant to see a boy lying in the boat, reading.

"This is private land, you know—didn't you see the notices?" Cosmo said, rather sharply—his voice was sharper because, for a moment, he had hoped that the boy was Con, but of course he wasn't.

With considerable reluctance, the boy shut his book and slipped it into a pouch that dangled from his belt. He looked up at Cosmo, frowning short-sightedly. He had a rough, uncared-for appearance—greyish skin, fuzzy, no-coloured hair, bony hands, a few spots—no one would ever pick *him* out of a crowd for his promising looks; if he were in a basket with a lot of mugs, they would be marked "seconds". His teeth were discoloured from neglect—like Bun's, Cosmo thought—and his voice when he spoke, was a croak, as if he had not used it for some time.

"I ask your pardon. I hoped that you would come this way. That was why I waited here. I thought no harm. If I have offended—forgive me."

His voice was quite different from what Cosmo had expected; rough, with some kind of country accent, but very polite—rather humble, in fact.

"Waiting for *me*? I'm sorry—I didn't—" Now Cosmo felt embarrassed, felt that he had been rude. But the boy was such a poor dismal-looking sort of erk, with his big hands and feet, his shabby, nondescript clothes, and his doubtful, propitiating look—like Bun again—Cosmo couldn't help wishing that he would go away. He looked dull—that was the trouble. "Did Mr Marvell tell you to come?" Cosmo asked, thinking ungratefully, I'm lonely, but not for *this* kind of company. I'd far sooner be on my own!

"They said I could learn from you. So I have come to

ask you to teach me. They said you would know me. I am Sim," the boy said as though that explained everything. "I have brought my things," he added hopefully, pointing to a pile on the river-bank which Cosmo had taken for some old bits of rusty iron thrown out by Mr Marvell. But, looking closer, he saw there was a kind of tunic, and leggings, of chain-mail; a dented helmet shaped like Mrs Tydings's jam cauldron, also rusty; and some terrible-looking contraptions that might be spurs.

Now Cosmo was really taken aback. "*Teach* you?" he stammered. "Wh-what am I supposed to teach you? Geometry — stuff like that?"

"Nay, no magic. I am a very plain fellow." And indeed Sim looked it. "Though I am fond of books," he admitted. "I was sorry when my father took me from the monastery."

"What have I got to teach you, then?"

"Why, to fight. I am going on the crusade, you see. Next month. With my uncle Aveyron, my mother's brother. We are going to rescue the city of Jerusalem." Sim heaved a sigh, as if he did not relish the prospect.

"Why go," Cosmo said, "if you don't want to?"

"Oh, I must. My father bound me into my uncle's service. He owed my uncle for a piece of land — so my service is a means of paying that debt. — I must learn to manage a boat — for we shall be travelling over the sea — and to fight."

"Oh, well, I can teach you to row, anyway. That's not hard. We may as well start now, if you like. The oars are in the shed — do you want to help me get them down off the beams?"

Poor Sim was as clumsy as he looked, all thumbs — twice he was nearly knocked out by loose planks while they were taking down the oars, and then he slipped and fell into the water – but he took these misfortunes with unruffled good humour, laughing at himself for being such a jackass. It turned out that he could not swim, either, so Cosmo had to teach him the rudiments of that – though the water was icy, much too cold for bathing really, and would be for several weeks yet. Still, you could hardly let the poor wretch go off to the crusades in such a state of ignorance and incompetence.

"Keep your blades *down*, Sim! You'll knock yourself cold if you wave them about in the air like that. Okay; take a rest now – let them trail back along the boat. – Why isn't your father going on the crusade?"

"Oh, he went once before, when he was younger. When my uncle Robert was killed. That was how my father inherited the Manor – he was the second brother, you see."

Cosmo did see.

"And you are your father's eldest son?"

"Ay. But he has never loved me," Sim said resignedly. "He put me into the monastery when I was six. And indeed I would have been glad to stay there. A monkish life would be no hardship to me. Now that my younger brothers are growing, my father will have enough help at the Manor."

"Did – has anyone ever told you about a prophecy?" Cosmo delicately avoided the word *curse*. But Sim looked wholly blank and bewildered.

"Father Anselm holds that prophecies are vain and wicked things, coming from the Devil. I know nothing concerning any prophecy."

"Oh, well, forget it."

Now Cosmo felt really angry – he was not quite sure with whom. Fancy sending this poor simpleton off on a crusade, though! He hardly knew enough to come in out of the rain. Certainly didn't know what was in store for him.

Nor, presumably, did the uncle who had taken his service as payment for a debt.

"What kind of fighting do you have to learn?"

"Why, with sword and spear—what else?"

No use expecting people to use net and trident in the Holy Land, Cosmo supposed.

"Well, Mr Marvell lets me ride his young horses—I suppose we could have a try at jousting. We'd better bring your armour along—it's in a shocking state—you can't go off to Jerusalem with it all rusty like that! It'll all have to be scrubbed with a metal brush. But first we'll soak it in something to get the worst off. Good grief, man, it's *heavy*!—and you're expected to wear that in the *desert*?" He imagined trudging through the Australian desert weighed down by all those heavy iron rings. They were flat, about the size of halfpenny pieces, overlapping, sewn to a thick leather jacket, which, in itself, must have weighed five or six pounds.

Cosmo discovered that Sim hardly knew how to ride, even. He explained that there had been little opportunity in the monastery, save when, very occasionally, he had been sent on an errand, riding the choirmaster's ambling mule. Astride of flighty Juno he fell off more often than he stayed on, so Cosmo transferred him to the more sober and biddable Punch.

"I wonder what you'll be riding, out there in the desert?"

"My uncle plans to take six chargers with him. Some knights wait, until they reach Acre, and there buy Saracen steeds—but they are poor spindly things, my uncle has heard, not fit to carry a man of substance. These are more like his horses," and Sim looked respectfully at the massive Blossom, whose enormous hoofs needed shoes the size of barrel-hoops.

Perhaps it was as well that Mr Marvell was away today, buying seed at some superior agricultural supply store in Reading. Cosmo was not certain if he would have approved of the exercise Punch and Juno were receiving – though they seemed to enjoy it thoroughly.

"Keep your legs as straight as you can, Sim," Cosmo panted – remembering the knights in the Bayeux tapestry with their feet almost touching the ground. "And sit *back* – not so far forward. Keep your centre of gravity in your seat, man!"

"I cry your pardon? I know not this centre of gravity."

They were tilting at each other with long ash-poles, which were not really heavy enough, the points tended to fly up in the air. Cosmo presently had the notion of wiring old pound and two-pound weights, from a rusty set of scales that he had found in the old dairy, on to the ends. Then the points kept down satisfactorily but were rather damaging if, as occasionally happened, they connected with the target. After a while Cosmo had another good idea – he rigged up a punchbag made from a big plastic agricultural sack stuffed with insulating wool and suspended from a bough of the great oak in the middle of the pasture.

"Pretend that it's a Saracen – no, go on, you've *got* to, Sim!" he shouted. "If you don't spike him, he's going to spike you."

"I was not made for warfare," poor Sim gasped, as Punch cantered to a ponderous halt.

"What *are* you good at?"

"Why, nothing," Sim said humbly. "But Brother Lawrence said I have good perseverance." He pronounced it per-*sev*erance.

Cosmo had to admit this was true. Sim was prepared to go on trying as long as he was asked to; but presently, for the sake of the horses, they had to stop, and walk Punch and Juno till they stopped sweating and were ready to be rubbed down. Then the chain-mail – which Cosmo had left soaking in a bath of Clearust – had to be scrubbed and sanded. Mrs Tydings's wire stove-brush was some help there; so were wire pot-scourers. A good deal of skin came off their fingers too.

"What we really need," said Cosmo, "I'm sure they must have them in factories, is some kind of big tumbling-machine that would roll the stuff round in emery or against bristles until it's all scoured."

Failing this, they had to do it all by hand.

Here, however, Cosmo had to admit, Sim showed his merit as a companion. He might not be able to do anything else well, but he could sing in a clear tuneful voice, and knew all kinds of songs, from monastic chants and hymns to funny little jingles, some of which, he admitted with a blush, he had made up himself.

> "My beautiful sister Alice
> Deserves to live in a palace
> Her hair is bright as the golden fleece
> And the troubadours call her Bele Alys."

"The words are pretty silly, Sim," said Cosmo kindly, rubbing away at a legging. "But the tune is first-rate."

"I can play on a lute a little, too," Sim offered. "The choirmaster had one. But of course," he added sadly, "you can't take a lute on a crusade."

Cleaning the armour proved a four-day job. The Clearust, as Cosmo had predicted, only took off the worst; after that it was a case of steady rubbing, with a bit of sword practice in the afternoons. At the end of each day, Sim was so exhausted that he seemed to go out like a candleflame.

Cosmo was pretty tired too but he supposed he must have more stamina – poor Sim looked as if he had never eaten a full meal in his life.

Just the same, Cousin Eunice, emerging from her proofs, said, "Are you all right, Cosmo? We hardly seem to see you."

"Oh, yes, I'm fine," he said. "It's just – there's a job I've got to do."

"Well, don't *overdo* it."

By Friday the armour was reasonably bright. They had given up over the spurs – wicked, spiked things, with enough rust on them to give any horse gangrene. "I'd leave them behind, honestly, Sim," Cosmo said. "You're not the world's best rider – one jab with those and your horse'll have you into the Dead Sea."

Then they did some bow-and-arrow practice. Cosmo suspected that this might be more useful than all that spear stuff – he had heard that the Saracen attack was a kind of guerrilla warfare, darting over the sand-dunes, sending off a flight of arrows, and galloping away into the distance again.

Unfortunately Sim was a hopeless shot. He could not seem to hit anything that was smaller than a door, or farther than three feet away.

"You need glasses, pal."

"Glasses?"

"Spectacles."

"I know not spectacles."

The poor boy was desperately short-sighted. When he read his little book, *Lives of the Saints*, he held it three inches from his nose.

"Anyway," Cosmo reflected, "I suppose you could

hardly wear glasses under that saucepan. Put it all on, Sim, and let's see how you look."

So, piece by piece, the armour was all hung or jammed on to Sim; the short tunic, or hauberk, with sleeves coming down to the wrists and chain-mail gloves to match; the leggings, or chausses, also of chain-mail sewn on to cloth, and the eye-slitted helmet which when put over his head suddenly turned the inoffensive Sim into a highly sinister figure.

"There ought to be a shield, a sword, and a spear, of course," he said. "But those my uncle will provide."

Cosmo had forgotten about the shield.

"Blimey—that as well! How much does the shield weigh? Ten or twelve pounds at least; *and* the sword; you had better do some weight-lifting exercises, Sim, to thicken up your biceps. Like this, see, twenty or thirty times every morning and evening."

Sim heaved another long sigh.

"You know not, friend, how fortunate you are to dwell in this peaceful spot, and not be required to ride off and rescue the Holy places from the infidel."

"Oh, I do know, pal," Cosmo answered sadly. "I do know; believe me. Are you all fixed up now? Want a trial fight, with staves, to see how you manage in your armour?"

"I thank you, no." Sim was firm. "There will be fighting enough by and by. And you have been too good a friend these last few days for me to wish to fight you any more— even in play! God keep you. When I come back—" his voice wavered for a moment—"when I come back from the crusade I shall visit you again, and shall have great tales to tell, and many trophies to show!"

"Of *course* you will," said Cosmo, feeling as if his heart was breaking. Twilight was beginning to thicken. He said,

"Is your uncle going to come and pick you up here, or what?"

"I am to meet him, this eve, at the head of the lane, where it meets the causeway. So I had best be off. Adieu, my good, good friend and helper. When two grown men bid farewell, they think no shame to embrace," he said, and hugged Cosmo, nearly tipping himself over. Then he stumped away at a slow but dogged pace, swaying slightly from side to side, but each time just managing to recover his balance.

Cosmo watched him vanish into the twilight, and heard his small clear voice raised bravely in one of his own songs:

"See the crusader
Stride up the lane.
He will be a hero
When he comes again.
Gallant are they
Who now have gone
With helmet and sword
To Ascalon.
If he be not
In battle slain
He will be a hero
When he comes again."

7

Moley

"Do you happen to know whether that monkish chronicle mentioned if there was a Simon Curtoys killed in the crusades?" Cosmo asked Eunice at breakfast one day.

"I don't remember, Cosmo. But it seems awfully likely, doesn't it? There was appalling mortality on those crusades anyway – about fifty per cent of those who went never came back; and on the earlier, more disorganized ones, I believe it was more like ninety per cent. No wonder the ones who came back were so pleased with themselves that they lie on their tombs with their legs crossed."

"Poor Simon. I suppose he did get killed."

"Poor Simon," echoed Eunice. "Where did you find him?"

"In my mind, I think. I've been having – dreams, about people."

"I wondered if something was going on. You've been – well, rather *absent* lately."

Cosmo looked at his cousin nervously. Eunice was a scientist; could she possibly believe in what had been happening to him? He did not think he could tell her; not just yet. He needed to get himself sorted out first.

She went on, giving him a cautious glance, "Dreams are usually memories; the computer in your mind pressing a button, selecting something it wants to show you, that it reckons is important. Do you know, I read somewhere, that we use more energy suppressing things we want to forget than in remembering things we want to keep. Isn't that strange?"

"Do you think," said Cosmo, "that my computer could press a button in somebody *else*'s mind? Someone who had been dead for hundreds of years? Or that his computer could press a button in my mind?"

Eunice looked at him gravely. "I don't see why not," she said. "Telepathy is a very well-established fact by now. People are getting in touch with each other's minds all the time. And I wouldn't think that an interval of a few hundred years could make much difference. Listen—" she switched on the radio, which, at that moment, happened to be playing a Mozart bassoon concerto. "We are hearing that *exactly* the way Mozart heard it in his mind, just about two hundred years ago. It's just as if he is transmitting his idea to us. So, if a tune, why not other things? Pictures, sensations, tastes, ideas, other kinds of sounds? Formulae? We have to remember too that our five senses—sight, hearing, feel, taste, smell—are a *terribly limited* means of finding out what's going on around us. We're like deaf, colourblind, myopic bats groping about—dogs can smell things that we can't, owls can hear sounds our ears can't catch, telescopes can see objects far beyond our range of vision—heaven only knows what is happening right in front of our noses, which our primitive apparatus just isn't capable of grasping. We're like a little old lady with an ear-trumpet and a crystal set, trying to hear the London Philharmonic which is playing away at top volume in the next room." She looked at her watch. "Heavens, I must get on with my proofs. I keep forgetting that, just because *you're* on holiday doesn't mean that I'm off the hook. See you at lunch—" and she hurried off to her study.

Cosmo decided that now was the time to make a thorough exploration of the mill buildings. He had been rather ducking that—the insides looked so dark and cobwebby and Eunice said the floors were rotten; and he had really been quite occupied, one way and another.

As usual he couldn't resist standing on the footbridge and staring down into the clear fast-running waters of the Dribble. He thought about Con, and about Sim. Had he dreamed them, or made them up? Were they products of his own mind? How could he ever tell? They had seemed perfectly real. There, moored by the bank, was the boat in which Sim had been lying, reading his book; there, across the lawn, was the walnut tree, the look-out platform defended by the poles that Con had helped hammer into place. Surely they were real people? If I had made them up, if I had invented them, he thought, I'd have liked them more from the start, I would have made them into ideal friends. But I didn't like them, not at first. And then, later, I found out things about them that I hadn't expected—so they must have been real, mustn't they?

Soon he would tell Eunice about them. But not just yet.

All of a sudden, he decided that he didn't want to explore the mill today.

His decision was affected by an optical illusion he had had just for a moment or two. A few semi-rotten planks were leaning against a wall of the mill building. For a brief flash of time he had been certain that he saw a man in a black cloak standing there, motionless, watching him. Then he turned his head a bit more and realized with relief that what he had seen must have been the triangular dark shadow of the planks against the wall. But still – the mill would keep for another day. Instead he did various jobs for Mr Marvell, helping him sink two posts and make a gate for the pigsty.

After lunch Mrs Tydings said she was going to walk over the fields to Gitting-under-Edge to visit her cousin who kept the shop there; she asked if Cosmo would like to go along. He hadn't been that way yet, and said that he would. They set out together wearing raincoats and Cosmo carrying a basket which contained a cake Mrs Tydings had made for her cousin.

The diagonal path they took climbed through the wood behind the house. Bluebells were beginning to come out but were still half curled up; the general effect was like a greenish grey mist through the wood. Halfway up, Cosmo noticed a tremendously strong smell of garlic; looking down he saw that they were above the point where the brook bubbled out of the hillside as a spring, and began its descent.

"Ransoms growing down there," said Mrs Tydings.

"Ransoms?"

"Wild garlic. See those white flowers? Keep off a peck of vampires, those would," Mrs Tydings said with her sniff, and Cosmo chuckled, thinking of Remove's nickname for Eunice. If they knew what she was really like!

"How are you getting on at school, then?" asked Mrs Tydings, as they came out from the top of the wood. In front of them, now, stretched a long smooth ridge of ploughed land which they would have to cross. It was like walking over the back of a whale, high and windy, with gulls and plovers wheeling around them. Their path went ahead in a series of right-angle turns, working round the edge of fields. The sky was grey and flurried, undecided whether to rain or not.

"School? Not too well. The work's all right but I don't like the people. They're spiteful."

"Ah. They're like chicken, I daresay," Mrs Tydings said. In spite of her age she had no trouble keeping up with Cosmo, she walked with the loose stride of a country-woman. "You keep chicken cooped up, they take to pecking theirselves and each other. Children's the same. I don't hold with boarding schools. It's not natural to take children from home. But I daresay they'll get better, you'll find, as they get bigger."

"Mrs Tydings," Cosmo said, hopping over a style – ahead of them, across a pale-brown horizon of curved ploughland, they could now see the steeple and roofs of Gitting-under-Edge, a small hamlet huddled against a grassy hillside.

"Well?"

"Do you think the Curtoys family curse will ever stop?"

"You been worrying your head over that?"

"Of course I have! What about when *I* grow up and have children?"

"Well: I think it *will* stop in the end," said Mrs Tydings, after some thought. "Trouble is, when someone gets real furious, like that old priestess must have been – and you can't blame her, poor soul, with her daughter and her grandson killed – you get someone real vicious-angry like that, what they're going to do's going to have an effect for a long, long time. It's like dropping burning acid on cloth – it don't go through only one layer, it goes down and down. But it won't go on for ever; in the end it'll come to a thicker layer of cloth, maybe, and there it'll stop."

"You think it'll be like that with the curse?"

"Ah, I do."

"What sort of thing might stop it, do you think, Mrs Tydings?"

"Well," she said matter-of-factly, "maybe what your Ma and brother done might stop it. Going off by theirselves like that. Breaking the pattern, putting in another kind of layer. Do you see what I mean?"

And immediately, Cosmo *did* see what she meant. He looked at her in amazement, thinking that her shrewd little wedge-shaped face was exactly right for the sort of person she was. An eight-foot patch of sunlight came sweeping towards them along the ground. Cosmo felt like bounding right over it, from end to end.

"Look – the sky's clearing," he said. "I believe the sun will be out by the time we walk home – see that big chunk of blue over there!"

When Cosmo went to bed that night he was comfortably tired – not exhausted, as he had been after days of armour-polishing and battle practice with poor Sim, but just pleasantly stretched by the things he had been doing, and the walk to the village. He fell asleep instantly, and began to dream at once.

He dreamed that Mark had shut him in the dog-kennel; they had had a dog once, long ago, in Hampstead.

"Mark, let me out. Please, *please* let me out!"

But Mark would not.

Trying to struggle out of his dream, Cosmo woke himself up. But then he realized that he must still be dreaming. Mark used, long ago, to have a horrible trick of holding Cosmo pinned under the bedclothes, the sheets and blankets pressed down tightly over his head so that he couldn't escape – it was the worst torture in the world.

Mark was doing it now. Cosmo tried to yell, but there was so little air in the black cave of the bed that he couldn't draw enough breath into his lungs to make any sound. He was suffocating. It was a horrible, nightmarish feeling. It must be a nightmare. And yet he couldn't break out of it. He tried to move his arms and legs, but they wouldn't move. A terrific weight, on top of him, was pressing him down. In fact the only reason why he wasn't squashed flat was that his bed had a hammocky sag in the middle; huddled in this dip, with his head jammed between his arms, he was just able to survive. But not for long ... Again he tried to call out, but could only produce a grunt.

It *must* be a nightmare!

"Cosmo!"

That was Eunice, her voice cracked with horror and amazement. "What in heaven's name – Cosmo, are you all right under there? Are you there?"

"Ugh – "

"*Wait*, I'll have to fetch Emma – Keep calm, Cosmo, I'll only be gone three minutes – "

It seemed like a century. By breathing shallowly, Cosmo reckoned he might manage to last for six more breaths. His eyes felt red-hot, his cheeks were swollen, he had a pain like a blade in his chest –

He had counted up to twelve when he heard Mrs Tydings.

"Good gracious *heavens*, Miss Eunice, how ever in the world did that get there?"

"I cannot imagine! But Cosmo's underneath, and we've got to get it shifted. Cosmo? Can you hear me?"

"Ugh – "

"We're going to lift it when I say one, two, three. Can you push up too? Kind of hump yourself? It's going to take all our combined strength to get it shifted. Do you understand?"

"Ugh."

"Okay. Get ready. One—two—*three! Lift!* Are you all right, Emma? For god's sake don't drop it again—tilt this way if you feel it going—good—heave—again—again—well done, Cosmo—*got it!*"

At last Cosmo was able to struggle out from under. The light was on in his bedroom he now realized—must have been before, but he had not been aware of it. Eunice and Mrs Tydings—the latter in her locknit nightgown and pink flannel dressing-gown, looking tousled and appalled—Eunice still in day-clothes but equally white and shattered-looking—were standing with their eyes fixed, not on Cosmo, but on the thing that had been on top of him.

It was the wardrobe.

Not a small wardrobe. A big, old-fashioned oak one. It had probably stood at the end of his room for a hundred years. It weighed as much as a cart. Now it lay tilted over the end of the bed, where, by pushing and levering, they had managed to slide it. Like a drunk man against a lamp post.

It had been right on top of Cosmo.

"It's lucky the bed has such a sag in the middle," he said after a moment. "Otherwise I might really have been squashed."

"Are you sure you're all right?" Eunice said in rather an odd voice. She was still very pale.

Cosmo moved his arms and legs.

"Yes, I'm okay. My shoulders got a bit bruised. Luckily I was sleeping on my face with my head almost under the pillow; I mostly do. But what made you come? I couldn't shout for help. I hadn't any breath."

"I heard the crash. I *felt* it. The whole house shook."

Mrs Tydings was indignant.

"How could that blessed wardrobe have fallen on the bed? Just tell me, *how*? Had you been moving it around, Cosmo? Fiddling with it or shifting it?"

"Never touched it."

"That's a good twelve feet away! It didn't just fall! It must have flown. How are we ever going to get it back again?"

"Well, we can't shift it now, that's certain," Eunice said. She laughed a little, shakily. "It's going to take a team of strong men with ropes and levers to get it upright again. In the meantime, Cosmo, I think we'll make you up a bed somewhere else. But first let's all have a little brandy."

Lob was at the head of the stairs, whining and bothered about the whole affair. He followed them down and huddled against Eunice as she poured the brandy. "I don't blame you," she said to him. "I feel the same myself!"

"Could there have been an earth tremor?" suggested Cosmo.

He tried the brandy, which he had never tasted before; it was like fiery vanilla, he decided; not a particularly pleasant taste, but certainly very hot and heartening when it got a little way down.

"If it was an earthquake," snapped Mrs Tydings, "why didn't nothing else fall over? That wardrobe's never been shifted in *my* lifetime."

Eunice looked at Cosmo in a worried way and said, "It seems as if you've disturbed something, Cosmo."

"What sort of something?" he said uneasily.

"Well—I don't really know. Something with a lot of energy."

"First time I heard there was energy in a wardrobe," sniffed Mrs Tydings.

"Maybe you'd better sleep the rest of the night in Emma's cottage. Would you mind, Emma?"

"Course not. He's welcome. But what about you, Miss Eunice? Won't you be nervous here on your own?"

"Where I've lived for twenty years? Not likely! I'll have Lob. Besides, I don't think this disturbance has anything to do with me. It's obviously Cosmo that sets it off."

"I'm very sorry," Cosmo said uncomfortably.

"Oh, don't apologize, my dear! It's tremendously interesting. Only, I think we'd better keep an eye on you for a day or two."

Sleeping in Emma's cottage was comfortable – like being inside an egg. The house was tiny, just two rooms up and two down – part of the long barn building. Cosmo's bedroom looked out on to a little cobbled yard at the side, where Mrs Tydings grew pinks, lavender, sage, and a camellia bush round the edges, besides pots of geraniums and begonias. He could hear the comfortable quacking of her ducks in the shed across the yard. From his other window, in the back wall, he could see the water-meadow and the fold of wood curving round to the river.

There was a trellised wallpaper on the wall, with bunches of roses, a picture of King George V wearing the Order of the Garter, and a soulful little girl looking up at a thrush.

Just the same, it took a long time to get back to sleep.

Next morning, Mr Marvell was brought in to inspect the fallen wardrobe.

"You don't hardly know what to make of a thing like that, do you?" he said, after surveying it for some time in silence. He did not offer any suggestions as to what might have caused it to shift twelve feet from its base and fall on Cosmo, but added thoughtfully, "You want her put back where she were before, Miss Doom? I could get a couple of the maintenance men down from the Place, I daresay, to help me do that."

"I think we'd rather get rid of it. What do you feel, Cosmo? You'd have a lot more space in your room without it, if you ever wanted to put up a model railway or anything of the kind."

Cosmo didn't think he would be wanting model railways. But he was happy at the suggestion of his permanent residence at the mill house that Eunice's words seemed to hold. And he was perfectly definite in his feelings about the wardrobe.

"I'd sooner get rid of it, thank you."

"Can't say I blame you. Well, Mr Marvell – can it be got out?"

Mr Marvell measured it with his eyes.

"Not in one piece," he said. "That must have been put together in here. Beautiful oak. Cut up a treat, that will. You could make yourself a nice dresser or half a dozen coffee tables."

"Oh well, we'll think of something."

"Maybe there's a skeleton in it," Cosmo said hopefully. It still gave him a very queer feeling to see the massive piece of furniture leaning drunkenly against the end of his bed. There *must* have been an earthquake. How, otherwise, coult it have got there?

Slightly to his disappointment he was not encouraged to, help with the dismantling of the wardrobe.

"Just indulge me in this, will you, Cosmo?" Eunice said. "I can't avoid a nervous feeling that it might fall on you again while it was being taken to pieces – or that you'd get your leg accidentally sawn off, or some other little mischance. – I have to go into Oxford to leave my proofs

131

at my publishers – would you like to come along? I don't have to see my editor till two – we could do some sightseeing in the morning and have lunch out."

So the morning was spent cheerfully in looking at college gardens and going up the Radcliffe Camera and Magdalen Tower, followed by lunch at the Mitre.

While Eunice was visiting her editor, Cosmo went into Blackwells bookshop; and there he was surprised to run into the pale, self-contained Moley, also browsing among paperbacks.

"Hullo!" Cosmo said unguardedly, forgetting the feud in his surprise. "What are you doing in Oxford?"

"Hullo yourself." Moley did not sound particularly hostile; quite amiable, in fact. "Why shouldn't I be here? I live in Oxford."

"Well then – if you live here, why in the world are you a boarder?"

Moley said calmly, "I'm a boarder because I like it better."

"You'd rather *board* than live at home?" Cosmo was thunderstruck.

"Dear me, yes," Moley drawled. "You see my parents are divorced, and I don't greatly care for my stepmama who lives here in Oxford with my Dad – let alone my dear, sweet, angelic little stepbrother and sister. Also I'm supposed to have a wonky ticker, you know – " he thumped his skinny chest – "and old Doc Hobson said there would be less general *wear and tear* if I were residing at school, under *controlled conditions*, you know. Conditions at my father's house are sometimes a bit uncontrolled."

Cosmo hardly knew what to say. He was greatly startled at this new light on Moley's home-life, and felt sympathetic too. After a moment he asked,

"What about your own mother? Where is she?"

"Oh, well, she's an actress, you see, Lalage Bosworth – "
even Cosmo, coming from so far away, knew that name –
"so she's mostly off somewhere making a film, or in a
play. But if she's working in London, where she has a
house, I go and stay with her there, in the holidays."

At this moment Eunice came into the bookshop accompanied by a thin, worried grey-haired man.

"Oh, there's my Da," Moley said. "He's not a bad old
stick, actually. But my stepmama has him trussed, trephined,
and hogtied, un-fortu-nately."

"There you are, Paul!" Moley's father gave him a
harassed, affectionate look. "Professor Doom and I have to
go back to her home to look through some extra material
that we think might have to go into her book. Do you want
to catch a bus home, or – " he glanced from his son to
Cosmo to Eunice – "do you want to come along? Professor
Doom has kindly suggested it."

"Do come, Paul, if you'd like," Eunice said. "It would be
fine for Cosmo to have some company."

This invitation made Cosmo very nervous. Would
Moley think that pressure was being put on him to visit the
form pariah? Did he himself want Moley to come?

Moley appeared rather hesitant, but perhaps the mill
seemed preferable to his stepbrother and stepsister; after a
moment's thought he said, "Thanks, I'd like to come."

It was decided that Moley should drive out with Cosmo
and Eunice, while Professor Molesworth went back to his
office for a spare set of Eunice's proofs. On the drive out
Eunice was unexpectedly funny, describing for Moley's
benefit, how, in the days when she had still been teaching at
a school, she had taken a party of advanced A-level maths
students on a working holiday, staying at a ruined Scottish
castle, which had turned out to be the storage-place of an

illicit whisky-still, and her students had become involved with the whisky-runners.

"I began to wonder why their maths was getting better and better but also wilder and wilder – they seemed to be grasping concepts that I'd have thought were far out of their reach; and then I went out to dinner with the local Laird and his family, and when I got back the students and the whisky-runners were having a great party, playing sardines all over the castle and hunting in the dungeons for the square root of minus one, which somebody swore they had seen down there."

Moley laughed uninhibitedly. "Were there any ghosts in the castle?"

"No, none. But we think we have acquired a poltergeist at Courtoys Mill House, don't we, Cosmo?" Eunice told the story of the wardrobe.

Cosmo, anxiously watching Moley's expression while she told it, wondered if Moley would suspect this to be yet another piece of family boasting or exaggeration; he wished that Eunice had not mentioned the wardrobe. But Moley seemed sincerely interested and astonished.

Cosmo could not help worrying too, slightly, about Moley's weak heart; suppose some other piece of furniture fell over while he was at the mill house? They had better stay out of doors as much as possible. – Although sad, it was also something of a relief that Con and Sim had gone – supposing Moley would have been able to see them. But very likely he would not.

One way and another, Cosmo felt very nervous about the visit, and wished it had not taken place. He was rather silent and constrained on the drive out, and afraid that both Eunice and Moley had noticed this.

Professor Molesworth, who had a nippy little Renault,

caught up with Eunice at the roundabout – she had been driving slowly – and after that both cars proceeded in consort and arrived together, the boys taking turns to open the gates.

As soon as they reached the mill house, Eunice and Professor Molesworth vanished indoors to work on the book.

A little half-heartedly, Cosmo began showing Moley round. They went to the island first, and looked at the weir and Cosmo's clearing. By now nettles and huge burdocks and teazles had grown across the mill entrance; Cosmo did not suggest going inside, and Moley did not ask to be taken in.

Then they went up-river a quarter of a mile in the skiff, with Cosmo at the oars, because rowing was one of the things forbidden to Moley. But it turned out that he was knowledgeable and enthusiastic about fishing and asked if he could come back for a day of it sometime. Cosmo felt rather sad in the boat, remembering poor Sim; after a while he stopped rowing, let them drift back to the moorage, and took Moley, instead, to see the farm buildings and the pigs who were now occupying their new quarters. Scratching the pigs' backs occupied some more time – the afternoon seemed to be dragging a bit, due to the fact that Cosmo was not certain what kind of things Moley liked doing, and Moley was being rather too polite.

In the barn they found Mr Marvell mixing pig-mash.

"There's your wardrobe," he said, nodding to a stack of massively thick oak boards. "We didn't find any skeleton in it, I daresay you'll be sorry to hear. All we found was a George III penny. You'd better have it for a luck-piece – keep you safe from anything else falling on you."

He fished it from his pocket. It was dated 1765, was very

thick, with a grooved edge, and the head of George wearing a wreath of laurel. Somebody had bored a small hole in it.

"You could wear it round your neck," Mr Marvell suggested, and threaded a piece of binder-twine through the hole.

This find cheered Cosmo, and he took Moley round the side of the house and showed him the look-out platform in the walnut tree.

"*Gosh*," said Moley enviously. "Did you make that? Gosh, what a place! I wish I could go up – but that's just the sort of thing I'm not allowed to."

"Oh, then you'd better not," said Cosmo hastily, feeling that it had been rather unkind to show it to Moley. But the last thing he wanted was to encourage any forbidden activity.

"You go up though – let's see you use those holds."

Cosmo scurried up the pitons – he was getting expert at this by now, had worked out the most economical movements for getting from each hold to the next, and could nip round and up the big serrated trunk almost as fast as a squirrel.

From the last piton he had formed the habit of launching himself up with a push, grabbing, as he did so, at the guard-rail post on the left of the entrance gap for a last pull-up. But today, when he did this, to his complete and disbelieving astonishment, a section of the rail simply crumbled away in his hand. He felt himself falling backwards.

Down below he heard Moley's startled yell.

"*Cripes!* Cosmo!"

Using muscles in his legs and thighs that he didn't know he had, Cosmo thrust himself sideways with his feet, just before they came away from the trunk of the tree. The sideways push was just enough to allow him to get one hand over a smallish branch, which he gripped with frantic strength, managing to use the time of his swing past it to hook his other hand up and over the branch. Once dangling by both arms he was all right; he swung his legs up over the branch and worked back to the trunk, inspected the defective guard-rail, and climbed down by way of the pitons.

"Wow!" said Moley. "That was quite exciting! What's the matter, have you got an enemy, or something? Or just suicidal tendencies?"

"I can't understand it," Cosmo said. Now that he was back on the ground, his knees felt as weak as milk; in fact he was shaking like a fool. "Mr Marvell and I went over those posts carefully. I'd have sworn that one was as solid as a rock. He said they'd last ten years."

"He sure was mistaken, chum. Look at that."

Moley had retrieved a bit of the piece that came away in Cosmo's hand. It was completely rotten – powdered and crumbling like a sponge-cake.

Cosmo was struck quite speechless. But after a minute or two he said,

"I *still* don't believe it. Mr Marvell looked at them all so carefully. And so did I. *None* of them were rotten."

Thinking it over he went on,

"I'd rather my cousin didn't get to hear about this, if you don't mind. She'd worry. After all, she's supposed to be in charge of me till my father gets to England."

And Father would be upset if he got back and found his other son had a broken neck.

"Whatever you say," Moley's tone was equable. "You'd better hide the evidence somewhere."

"I'll take that rail down and burn it later." Cosmo shivered. A light drizzle was beginning to fall; the afternoon had deteriorated. "Come on, let's go in. It must be about teatime, anyway."

In fact Mrs Tydings appeared in the doorway, about to ring the bell, as they walked up to it. Cosmo went across and threw his piece of rotten wood on to the log-fire that smouldered in the hearth.

Mrs Tydings had cleared the big refectory table and set one of her splendid teas on it. Moley ate all her home-made delicacies with enthusiasm.

"Much more than he eats at home," Professor Molesworth remarked, watching his son with a wistful eye.

"More than he eats at school," Cosmo said.

Cosmo himself found it hard to eat. When Mrs Tydings scolded him he said defensively, "Well, we had lunch out."

After tea, Eunice and the Professor went back to work in her study, and, as it was now raining steadily. Moley and Cosmo got out the box of ivory pieces and played chess on the tea-table. Cosmo was not a bad player – he played quite often with Eunice and beat her occasionally – but Moley was better, making moves with great dash and imagination. He won four games to Cosmo's two.

"You ought to try playing against my cousin," Cosmo was saying, "I think you'd be pretty equally matched – " when they heard a loud crash from upstairs, followed by a series of thumps, as if one of the horses, Prince or Blossom, were walking heavily across the upstairs landing.

"What the dickens – ?" began Moley, and Cosmo said, "Oh, heavens, *now* what – ?" while Mrs Tydings, coming in with a bag of her home-made flapjacks for Moley because he had enjoyed them so much, exclaimed,

"Lawks! Did you ever!"

She was looking past the boys at the stairs which led down into the room where they were sitting. Cosmo spun round just in time to see his bed negotiate the turn round the banisters and come tobogganing down, all by itself apparently, the legs on their castors sliding heavily from step to step, thumpity-thumpity-thump.

Eunice and the Professor, startled to death at the noise, which was like houses falling down, came dashing from the study and witnessed the bed clatter down the last four steps and come to a stop, still right way up, on the brick floor. Even the bedclothes were still in place, though somewhat disarranged as the mattress had slipped down against the bedhead.

"*Well!*" said Eunice.

Professor Molesworth was highly suspicious.

"Did you boys rig that up? With a rope or something?"

"No, *honestly*, Da, we didn't," said Moley, who was suffocating with laughter, leaning back helplessly in his chair. "P-p-please, P-professor Doom, c-can I come to tea every week? I've n-never had such a good time in my life! N-no wonder Cosmo isn't very keen on school if he has all these larks going on at home!"

Eunice gave Cosmo a sharp look and said, "You didn't pull the bed down, Cosmo? You swear you had nothing to do with it?"

"You know I didn't. I've been with you all day – or outside with Moley."

"Yes – I know," she said. "Well, as you can see," she told the Molesworths, "we have a slight case of poltergeist."

"It really is remarkable," said Moley's father. He inspected the bed carefully, then went up to look at Cosmo's room, from where it had travelled by itself. "For a start," he said accusingly, "it couldn't have got through the door unless the legs had been unscrewed first."

"Oh, why boggle at a little thing like that?" said Eunice.

Moley began singing to the *Miller of Dee* tune:

> "Lets spend the day at Courtoys Mill
> It's really jolly there,
> Where wardrobes made of solid oak
> Come floating through the air
> And beds as well as naughty boys
> Toboggan down the stairs."

"I'm glad you're enjoying yourself," said Eunice tartly – Cosmo could see that she liked Moley though – "but how are we going to get the bed back again, just tell me that?"

"If I were you," said Professor Molesworth thoughtfully, "I wouldn't be in a hurry to put it back just yet. I'd wait till this disturbance settles down. Otherwise it might well just happen again."

Eunice sighed. "I daresay you are right. I can see that in the end we shall have all the furniture down here on the ground floor. Or chopped in pieces outside."

Cosmo's bed was put in the garden-room, and Eunice told him that he had better continue to sleep in Emma's cottage until things had settled down in the mill house.

"Would you consider getting in an exorcist?" Professor Molesworth suggested to Eunice. She looked doubtful.

"The trouble is, I don't think that *I'd* believe in lighting candles and drawing circles on the floor. And if it doesn't convince *me*, why should it convince the poltergeist? No, I think we'll just have to sweat it out. I'm sorry this visit has been a bit disturbed, Norman."

"Oh, don't apologize; Paul and I wouldn't have missed the experience for worlds, would we, Paul?"

"It's been terrific," sighed Moley. "I haven't laughed so much since Granny locked herself in the pantry on Boxing Day."

"Well you'd better come here for a weekend some time," Eunice said. "When things have settled down a little."

As the father and son were about to depart, Professor Molesworth, on the point of getting into the car, stopped to have a last word with Eunice about a footnote. While he did this, Moley said to Cosmo in a low voice,

"I say, I know you don't want to worry your cousin with the business about your tree house, but, honestly, I should watch out if I were you."

"I'm certainly going to," Cosmo said. "Thanks."

"Actually," Moley said, "I didn't mention it in there in case I was speaking out of turn but I shouldn't be surprised if that skinny old girl in black had something to do with it. Is she your grandmother? She was giving you an uncommonly old-fashioned look when we were playing chess."

"Old girl in black?" Cosmo gaped at Moley. "What old girl? You don't mean Mrs Tydings?"

"No, no, the other one. The old girl in black," Moley repeated patiently. "I thought she might be your grandmother because she's a bit like you. She came swanning in with a shawl over her head while we were playing chess, and looked over your shoulder. Didn't you notice her?" he said, observing Cosmo's blank expression. "I didn't take much of a shine to her, I must say. She looked just the type to think that locking somebody up and starving them to death would be a real laugh-riot."

"No, I didn't notice her," Cosmo said. "But I'll keep a look out. Thanks for mentioning it."

8

Osmond

"I LIKED YOUR FRIEND MOLESWORTH," Eunice said, when the father and son had left. "He's got a witty tongue."

"He's really more my enemy than my friend," Cosmo said absently. He was thinking, And not my only enemy, by any means.

He felt extremely uneasy.

Eunice was troubled too. She said, "Cosmo, I'm wondering if we'd better find somewhere else where you could stay for a bit."

He was horrified. "Go away from here? Oh, *no!*"

"You like it here?"

"Yes!" His reply was heartfelt.

"We do have a problem, though! Professor Molesworth and I were discussing it. You see— please don't take this wrong, but these occurrences, wardrobes and beds going on the rampage, have only begun happening since you came to the mill house."

Cosmo was embarrassed. "You mean, I'm making them happen?"

"Oh, not on *purpose*, of course," she said quickly. "But

things like that do happen sometimes with boys – people of your age."

"But in that case, don't you suppose it might happen wherever I went?" Cosmo said, trying to be detached about it, though in fact he found the idea quite foul – it was like having some disgusting disease, fits or something. "Besides – if I left the mill, where would I go?"

"Well, for instance, Professor Molesworth said you were welcome to go and stay at their house in Headington."

"Oh, no – thank you." He thought of the biting things Moley had said about his stepmother and her children. "Besides – suppose wardrobes started falling about *there*?"

"I have an idea they wouldn't. I think these – these phenomena are brought on by a combination of this place and your presence in it."

"Well, then," Cosmo said craftily, "don't you think it would be rather a shame not to – to make a scientific observation of what happens? It seems such a good opportunity."

Should he tell Eunice about Con and Sim? But he would really prefer to wait until he had his own ideas a bit more sorted out.

"Well – yes," she said, in a dubious manner. "But not at the cost of some awful accident. After all, we haven't only you to consider. I daresay you'd be able to take anything that came in a spirit of scientific curiosity and detachment." Cosmo wasn't quite so sure about that, he hadn't felt in the least detached when he was swinging twenty feet up by one hand. "But there's also your father to consider, and old Emma. She's in her seventies, we wouldn't want her bashed by a clock falling on her or anything of the kind."

"No, I do see." He was very cast down. "I do see it isn't fair."

"Perhaps we'd better wait two or three days and see how it goes." Eunice was obviously swayed quite a bit by his horror at the thought of going away. "We'll do a lot of careful observation. If you try to study poltergeists they tend to lay off their activities. Only do be careful, will you? Stay away from danger-points, and – and hold on to the banisters when you go downstairs."

Cosmo promised to do this, and went away to his own room – which looked remarkably bare now, bereft of bed and wardrobe. It did seem as if something – somebody? were trying to show him that he was not welcome in the mill house. He very much wished that he, too, had seen the skinny old girl mentioned by Moley. Who could she possibly be? And how dared she try to get him out of the mill house, where he had a perfect right to be? He'd like to give her a sock on the jaw, interfering old witch. Could she be connected with Con or Sim – one of their mothers, perhaps? It would be hard, he supposed, if you knew your son was going to be killed in battle, to see one of the younger brothers who didn't come under the curse. – But Sim and Con had not been hostile. Well, Con had been a bit surly at first, but that had worn off as soon as he saw that Cosmo intended to help him. Con and Sim had needed his help, of course – that was the difference. Perhaps this old girl only needed some kind of reassurance. It was hard, though, to reassure somebody you could not see. Strange that Moley had seen her and he had not: a reversal of the situation with Con and Sim, who had been visible to him but not to Eunice, Emma, or Mr Marvell. What did that mean? That the old girl didn't *want* him to see her – that she was hanging around now, invisible to him? The thought was very disagreeable. He glanced round the room. There was nothing to be seen, and he settled down to write to

Meredith. Poor girl, he could really sympathize with *her* now; the pang he had felt when Eunice suggested his going away brought back her passionate cry – "Only *one week* in my *own home*."

"Dear Meredith," he wrote, "We have been having rather a peculiar time here. And in case you don't believe me, Moley can tell you that some of it really happened, as he and his father were here today and saw two of the happenings … "

How could a perfectly solid piece of timber turn so rotten, in the course of a week – less than a week – that it crumbled to powder in one's hand? Perhaps a thing like that could happen in a tropical land where they had termites – but in cool, orderly England?

He would have to go over every inch of his look-out platform before he felt safe venturing up there again; and even then he would not feel safe. In fact – with a sigh – he saw that was the kind of thing Eunice had in mind when she said "Stay away from danger-points." But in that case where *could* he go? Near the horses? Across the footbridge? Along the river-bank?

"I'm not going to be driven out," he said angrily, aloud. "So you can put that in your pipe and smoke it."

Silence answered his words. He finished the letter to Meredith, opened his diary, and wrote, "Trouble with wardrobe. Went to Oxford with Eunice. Moley & his father to tea. Bed came downstairs." About to close the diary, he paused, noticing that at the end of the week was another full moon; how quickly that moon had shot round from change to change. Perhaps Eunice was right and time did go at different speeds.

During the next six days there were no more upsetting

incidents – perhaps because of Cosmo's cautiousness and the extreme watchfulness of Eunice. As she had said, poltergeists are disinclined to perform if they are expected to; and whoever or whatever it was in the mill house that had thrown down the bed and wardrobe either did not want to be studied, or had decided to bide its time until the inmates were off their guard. In the meantime Cosmo tried to keep away from heights, and from heavy objects that could conceivably fall on him. He slept at night in Emma's little bedroom with its view over the meadow; this was going to be a great advantage at the end of the week, he reflected, on the night of the full moon; he would then have a grandstand view of the coach-and-six if it passed by.

On Friday night he took his alarm with him and set it for 3 a.m. Then he climbed into Emma's spare bed (which was even more hammocky and saggy than his own) and fell asleep.

He dreamed that Mark was holding his head in the washbasin and had the taps full on. The gushing of the water woke him; then he realized that it was the buzz of the alarm. He had put it under his pillow so as not to rouse Emma in the next room; even so, through the thin matchboard partition he heard her grunt and murmur in her sleep. Old people sleep lightly.

Cosmo had not undressed, except for taking off his shoes. He got out of bed, moved the chair over to the window, and curled up on it, watching and waiting. The little yard down below him was quiet and dark, wrapped in shadow; but the long pale stretch of the watermeadow looked like a lagoon, breathing up silvery drifts of mist, and, beyond, he could catch a gleam of the river itself. At the far right-hand corner the black wedge of wood came down like the tip of a nutcracker, where the old road sliced round the curve between hillside and river. And over it all the high, pale moon sailed, in a sky that seemed scrubbed bare by wind; there were very few stars to be seen.

I wonder if the coach makes a noise, Cosmo thought. The luminous hands of the clock told him that he still had five minutes to wait; supposing the coach arrived on time, that was to say. Were phantom coaches always punctual? And how long do they go on running? For ever? And if they cease running, do they stop abruptly, like axed trains, or fade away, every month a little paler, until they are quite gone? Or is it not the passing of time that controls their life-span, but the number of people who see them? Perhaps, thought Cosmo, if nobody sees the coach, then it isn't there, like the tree in the quad. He felt very wide-awake; all kinds of ideas were whirling through his head. About the old girl in black: could she make an appearance both inside and outside of the mill house, as Con had been able to do? Or did she always stay inside? About Moley – why had he been able to see her? Could it have something to do with his weak heart – the fact that he was a rather delicate boy, sensitive to all kinds of things besides ordinary sounds and sights, perhaps?

Whoooo, whoooo, called a big barn owl, and floated past the window on pale wings that glistened as they caught the moonlight. A fox barked, up in the wood, and a pheasant chickered. In the distance the sound of the weir was like sandpaper continuously rubbing on very smooth wood.

Suddenly the coach was there. He could see it across the meadow, over to his left, travelling along under the black slope of wood, outlined in dim light. It faintly sparkled; like cobwebs with dew on them. So did the horses, three pairs, spanking along at a silent canter. The whole equipage moved without any sound at all, skimming around the perimeter of the meadow.

Gosh! thought Cosmo. What a sight to see—what an extraordinary sight! He watched with held breath. He could hardly believe in his own luck. To think that this happened month after month, and nobody knew or cared, nobody looked at it—except Emma, if she happened to get up for a digestive tablet. Why, you'd think people from all over the world would be coming to look at a turn-out like that. You'd think travel companies would be running nightly tours and film companies would be trying to film it. He wondered if it would be possible to catch it with a camera. Another time he must try; but probably, because of the dark, a special exposure would be needed, and that would be a problem with the coach going so fast.

Then something struck him. "It's never been known to stop," Emma had said very positively. But now—it was slowing down. And, at the corner of the wood, it came to a total standstill. Cosmo thought he could even see faint puffs of steam from the horses' nostrils.

The door of the coach opened. And a passenger got out.

As soon as the black figure had stepped down, the door closed again, the horses tossed their heads, and the coach moved off, almost instantly disappearing round the curve of the wooded hillside.

But the passenger who had descended—a black figure in a long cloak, impossible to say whether it were man or woman—began to walk purposefully, at a brisk pace, along the river-bank, and vanished, almost at once, out of Cosmo's line of vision.

Cosmo did hesitate, then, for a moment.

But he told himself firmly, "If I don't go out now, if I

don't try to discover where that person has gone, I shall never, ever, be able to forgive myself. For the rest of my life I shall know that I am an utter coward. Also – which will be far worse – I'll know that I let a discovery go by that I might have made."

He grabbed his torch in one hand, his shoes in the other, and crept down the tiny steep stairs as fast as he dared. Even so he heard Emma mutter and call out as she turned over in her sleep. He replied with a mild, reassuring noise, slipped softly across her brick-floored kitchen, and out through the back door, which was always kept on the latch, never locked. Now – if he ran fast round the cartshed, he ought still to get a sight of the black-cloaked figure on the river-bank before he or she reached the footbridge and either crossed it, or turned in the other direction towards the house ...

At this point Cosmo reached the corner of the cartshed. For one moment of mixed relief and disappointment, he thought that the figure had vanished entirely. Then he saw it, motionless, in the middle of the footbridge, looking down at the river. Just like me, thought Cosmo, beginning to lope across the dewy lawn. As though the figure had heard his thought it lifted its head, swung round, and continued on over the bridge to the island.

It seemed to be carrying something.

By the time Cosmo had reached the bridge, his quarry was out of sight, somewhere on the island.

Dared he call out? He was not sure that he dared, because he simply couldn't imagine what kind of an answer might come back. His scalp crept a little; cold spasms ran through all his fibres; his skin felt icy.

Walking gingerly, feeling with each foot before he put it down, he reached the middle of the bridge.

"Come along, boy," said a cold voice. "I am waiting for you."

Ahead of him, close to the mill building, Cosmo saw the figure in the black cloak. Now he was certain that it was a man; he could not have said exactly why. The arrogant, thin shape of the head and face, perhaps; or the height and build. Though, in fact, the man was not so very tall; nor as large-framed as Mr Marvell. But he moved with a swift, springy stride, walking on rapidly towards the mill. When he reached the high tangled growth of nettle and burdock by the entrance he pulled out a blade and slashed, sharply, right—left—right—the shadowy green stuff toppled away on each side of him like cobwebs.

"Who are you?" called Cosmo shakily. Something frightened him about this character—a kind of suppressed rage, visible in his movements—but that kind of fright was a lot easier to bear than the absolute fear of the unknown which had filled Cosmo as he crossed the meadow. Even the sharp, rank smell of the cut nettles had something reassuring about it. With great caution he stepped over the stone threshold and into the mill.

"Who am I? That's none of your business. What does it matter to you who I am?"

"It does matter," Cosmo said obstinately. "Who are you? Where have you come from in that coach?"

"Where have I come from? I don't mind obliging you there." Cosmo thought he heard a short, mirthless laugh. "I've come from Medmenham, if *that* means anything to you."

It meant nothing.

"Medmenham?"

"The Hellfire Club, you young fool. Why do you suppose I know about you? Why do you suppose I have come here to meet you?"

"*Do* you know about me?" Startled, Cosmo added, "What do you know?"

"Oh, I know. More than you reckon."

All this time, the other had been moving on and away, through black-velvet dark, and Cosmo, feeling warily ahead of him with hands, feet, and a kind of extra sense, had been slowly following. The dark was complete. But now, suddenly, there came a splintering crash of wood falling on stone as something gave way; a great rotting double door had been thrust aside, and a white flood of moonlight poured into the big empty place, revealing high stone walls, a ceiling almost out of sight overhead, a dusty board floor, and, outside the door-hole, a section of huge weed-grown millwheel. The sound and smell of water was all around them.

Cosmo still found it hard to distinguish any features of the cloaked man, who stood with his back to the light. He was visible simply as a black shape, with a fuzz of pale hair. He set down his bag, or whatever it was he carried, and dropped his cloak on the floor. Now he appeared to be dressed in dark, close-fitting clothes, with a gleam of white at the neck.

"How do you know about me?" persisted Cosmo, stepping sideways in the hope of obliging the other to turn his face into the moonlight. When he did so, it was a shock, for his face was familiar, though Cosmo could not have told why, or where he had seen it before. Light-coloured locks falling over the brow; a long, sharp nose; thin, angry lips and thin cheeks which seemed to be overspread with blemishes – scars? pock-marks? The eyes were in shadow, nothing could be seen of them, but the general impression was of a younger person than Cosmo had thought at first – eighteen, nineteen, perhaps? An ugly, unfriendly, unlikeable face, but at least he was a real person, not a monster; as real as Con, real as Sim.

"*How* do I know about you? Because of what we do at Medmenham."

"What *do* you do?"

"Things you wouldn't understand, little boy! Necromancy, thaumaturgy, divination. We have clever people there, learned people; their studies go so dark and so deep that they can tell the future, yes, to the last grain of sand that will fall as the last pyramid crumbles away into nothing – "

"Why have you come here, then? Who are you?" Cosmo demanded again.

"I am Osmond Curtoys, boy. Does that name make you tremble?"

"No! Why should it?"

"Because I am the last of my kind that you will meet. Oh, I know you think you are something remarkable because you met those two stupid children – "

"You aren't so very old yourself," Cosmo said boldly.

"Old enough to settle *your* hash, my young gamecock. Come then, if you are so full of spirit – choose a sword."

"What?"

"Choose a sword!" Arrogantly, Osmond Curtoys pointed to the bag he had brought with him – it was rather like a golf-bag, Cosmo saw, which, unstrapped, proved to contain several swords. It must have been heavy to carry, he thought, almost mechanically selecting one, an épée with a long slender whippy blade and a French handle.

"On guard!"

"But – hey! Wait a minute! How do you mean, on guard? I've never done this kind of fighting – I haven't learned fencing!"

Mark and Ma had, however; she had been senior blade in her fencing club at college, and had taught Mark all the feints, lunges, parries, thrusts, counters, and recoveries that she could remember. Mark had taken to it with enthusiasm; and, sometimes for hours together, little Cosmo had sat watching.

"That is *your* bad fortune," said Osmond Curtoys callously, and lunged forward at Cosmo. A fierce flash of moonlight ran up his blade.

"You rotten cheat!"

Almost instinctively Cosmo knocked his blade aside.

"I wasn't ready for you—that's not fair!"

"*Fair?*"

The bright blade came zipping at him again, and Cosmo, hardly readier than he had been before, managed to deflect it by twisting his wrist, throwing it off to the right. Vaguely he began to remember the voices of his mother and Mark.

"That is *carte*—the fourth position of the wrist—from the French *quatre*—and this is *tierce*, the third position—Always oppose your blade with the other hand, keep yourself in balance. On your *toes*, Mark, keep your weight exactly poised, ready to move forward, or back, or to the side, but always under control; this, now, is a *botte coupée*, beginning in high *carte*, finishing in low *tierce*. Now let me see you do it ... *Forte*, that is the upper half of your blade, the stronger part; see, with that, I can knock your point aside every time ... Watch your button, Mark! There—it has fallen off."

But there were no buttons on these swords. The points sparkled in the moonlight, bright and deadly.

"Fair?" Osmond repeated. "There's no question of *fair* between us two."

"Why not?"

"Because the black priest at Medmenham looked into the scroll of the future for me — looked ahead to see what fate will bring — " Osmond lunged expertly, and his blade came within a centimetre of Cosmo's cheek, if Cosmo had not thrown himself, half staggering, with his legs tangled together, off to the side.

Already his knees were shaking, his arms were aching with the effort of being held up high.

"I don't understand at all. What black priest? Are you an elder son?" Cosmo panted, trying, in his turn, to make a lunge. Up to now he had been fighting entirely on the defensive, it was as much as he could do to oppose his blade, in one way or another, to all the darting, piercing thrusts that his adversary was delivering; the point of Osmond's sword seemed like a whole nest of hornets, ready to sting on every quarter.

"Elder son? I am an *only* son!" Osmond shouted angrily. "How do you think my mother would feel if I were to die?"

"I suppose she'd have to bear it like all the rest — "Cosmo gasped, jumping backwards out of reach, and then bounding forward, trying for a *flanconade*, a thrust at his opponent's side.

"She is a woman of deep learning, of much lore, not the kind to put up tamely with a bad fate. When I asked the black priest if I should die fighting like my forbears — "

Their blades clashed, engaged, then flung apart again.

"The old fool! I don't believe he knows half that he pretends to. He said my battle would be against a boy younger than myself — a boy from another time. He named you. *But I do not intend to die!* He said — if I escaped you — and you are an unskilled fighter — then I should be the first to break away from the curse. As my clever mother planned. Mother?" he said. "Are you there?"

"Don't worry, my dove. I am close enough," came the answer, in a thin, dry voice, like that of a parrot. Cosmo was horribly startled by its closeness, and by the unexpected glimpse of a woman, beside the big moonlit opening. She was on his right, or sword-arm side, and seemed to be edging in, steadily coming closer to him. He remembered Moley's description, "a skinny old hag in black" ... "she looked the type to think that locking somebody up and starving them to death would be a real laugh-riot." This one was old enough, and skinny enough, to fit that description, and her expression, what he could see of it, certainly did.

"Stand farther off! Or you're likely to get hurt!" Cosmo panted at her. But the woman only laughed, edging farther in.

Osmond said, "You can't hurt her, fool! She will not be hurt by your blade. My mother is a *striga*. She can fly through solid walls. She has taught me much of what I know." He too laughed, rather crazily.

Cosmo could not help being horribly distracted by the presence of the old woman at his elbow, creeping closer and closer. He thought he saw her pick something off the floor, and wondered what it could be. Next moment he realized that it was the cloak that Osmond had flung down; using it as Con had used his gladiator's net she swung it to and fro, trying to trip Cosmo.

"Two to one isn't fair!" Cosmo shouted angrily, jumping backwards from one of Osmond's fierce thrusts.

"You may as well give up now, stupid boy! I can take a man's heart out and leave a sawdust one in its place," the old woman hissed behind his right shoulder.

"Why don't you, then?" Cosmo flung back. "If you can work all that magic, why not *do* it?"

"Fair?" Osmond said. "Only fools expect life to be fair!" Pressing forward steadily, he darted his point straight at

Cosmo's breastbone. Cosmo could see it coming at him like a diamond and, even in that moment, he remembered the needle-shaped Females of Flatland and the author's comment, "A Female in Flatland is a creature by no means to be trifled with." I'm finished, he thought, but at least I remembered a joke just before I died.

Incredibly, though, the darting blade struck something hard under his shirt and glanced off sideways. The old woman let out a harsh cry of rage, and Cosmo seized the chance to leap backwards out of danger. But how long could he keep up this unequal fight? He ached and trembled with fatigue, sweat ran scalding into his eyes, the cold air on his tongue tasted sharp as pewter, and his heart, thudding away savagely inside his ribs, felt like some heavy piece of deck-cargo that is liable to break loose from its moorings at any moment and hurtle about the ship, doing untold damage.

I'll never win this fight, Cosmo thought coldly, because this man wants to kill me—intends, *has* to kill me—and I don't want to kill him. All I want is for the fight to stop. Perhaps if I were to try and knock him out with my hilt—

Snatching a handkerchief from his pocket he wrapped it round the blade of his weapon and, holding the sword by the blade, flexed his knees, preparing to spring forward and bring down the hilt on Osmond's head. But, as he crouched, something black and smothering came down over his head. The cloak, he thought. That old hag has blinded me with the cloak.

The impulse of his spring took her forward, and he felt that he was dragging the woman with him. He could hear her breath rasping behind his ear. Then that sound was drowned by another—a rustling creaking rumbling noise that rose in volume to a crashing roar—and the boards suddenly fell away from beneath his feet, he felt himself poised in mid-air, then falling, falling, falling.

Solid objects, chunks of masonry or wood, were cascading round him – a shower of fragments battered his head and arms. His head was still wrapped in the black cloth – he could see nothing – fighting to disengage himself he gasped as he suddenly plunged into icy, rushing water. No time, now, for thought. He kicked and struggled instinctively, but knew that he was going down deeper – he felt that he was being whirled and tumbled over and over, like a marble being bounced down a flight of stairs in a bucketful of suds. He had let go of the sword long ago, and had no notion what had become of Osmond or the horrible old woman – no time or strength to concern himself with them – he was wholly occupied in kicking and battling his way upwards, trying to combat the fierce pulling tugging undertow that was sweeping him onwards and down. If he didn't manage to get some breath into his lungs soon, he would die – he felt certain that death was only seconds away.

And then, at the last possible moment, silver light bathed his face and air, sharp and stinging like Eunice's brandy, rushed into his open mouth. He saw the moon overhead, silvery and calm. He was on the surface of the water, being hurled along like a twig, in a breakneck smother of white foam. All I have to do now is keep afloat, he thought hopefully, and in the end the current is bound to slow down and I'll be able to swim to the bank.

I have to keep afloat ...

But just then his foot caught in an underwater snag, and something heavy struck his head a crashing blow. The moon vanished from view, and he went down, again into darkness.

9

Eunice, Richard, Moley, Meredith

"WHAT'S THE HELLFIRE CLUB?" Cosmo muttered when he next opened his eyes. He was lying on a bed, and Eunice was standing beside him. Her hair was tousled, and she wore a windcheater over her pyjamas. Lob was panting heavily somewhere nearby.

"The *Hellfire* Club? Why in the world do you want to know that?" She thought for a minute and said, "It was in the eighteenth century – a group of people – young rakes mostly I think – who practised devil-worship and black magic, things like that. They wanted to live for ever. Where did you hear about that?"

But Cosmo had drifted away again. His bones and muscles, every part of him, ached almost unbearably, as if he had been put through a mincer and turned into shepherd's pie. It was really too painful to put up with; his head felt huge, like a globe full of red-hot coals, his tongue was the size of a doormat …

"Could I have something to drink," he tried to gasp, but nobody seemed to hear him. Without any particular effort he left his body and rose up above it. A very good trick. Why don't they teach *that* in school, instead of silly dodge-ball or lists of prime ministers?

Now he was in a green, mountainous land, with yellow lupins flowering, and grey birds wheeling overhead, and broad clear shallow rivers, where one could swim or wade for ever, picking up pebbles, each one more shining than the last ... Con was there, without his neck-ring, and Sim, no longer pale and worried. They ran races and sang songs together. Even Lob was there, young and agile, bounding in and out of the water like a puppy after thrown sticks. And over the glossy grass thundered Prince and Blossom, Duke, Duchess, and Queenie, kicking up their enormous heels. Larks were exclaiming endlessly overhead. Otters played follow-my-leader down the river-bank. And, on a green slope in the near distance, Mark and his mother sat reading. Soon they would look up and wave to him joyfully and come to greet him ...

"Now just put this under your tongue a moment," someone was saying.

"Oh do go away," Cosmo protested. "Can't you see I don't want to be disturbed just now? I don't want to leave this place!"

"You have to go this time," Con told him, and Sim said, "Never mind. We'll wait for you here."

With grief and extreme reluctance, Cosmo slid back into his body. It seemed to have shrunk since he had left it. I need a larger size, he thought. Must tell Eunice – go to Marks & Spencer –

The body felt cold and clammy, too, like a banana peel; ugh, horrible! They'd much better throw it away. He began to shiver, but somebody packed warm bedclothes round him. He was vaguely aware, in drifts of time, that things were done to him; he was washed, he was obliged to drink, he was given pills and made to swallow them.

"I'd much rather go back where I was," he objected muzzily.

"Well I'm afraid we don't agree," said his father's voice. "We want you here."

He opened his eyes.

"Dad! When did *you* get here?"

"Oh, I've been around," said Richard. He looked extremely thin and tired, greyer than Cosmo remembered; even his eyebrows were grey. He was not smiling, exactly, but there was a light behind his eyes that had not been there for some time. He took hold of Cosmo's hand, shaking it a little.

"Welcome home!" he said. "You gave us a bit of a fright."

Eunice came in with a beaker full of hot milk. She, too, was pale but calm.

"Here, get this down you," she said scoldingly to Cosmo, and, as he drank the disgusting stuff, "Well! You're a fine one! Just you wait till Emma starts laying into you!"

He looked around. Now he realized that he was back in his own room. When had they found time to dismantle the bed and put it up again? He saw, too, that some planks from the sawed-up wardrobe had been made into a kind of shelf-and-cupboard unit at the end of the room.

"Good heavens ... When was all that done?"

"Oh, there was time. We had you down in the garden-room at first."

"At *first* – ?"

"You had a touch of pneumonia," his father explained. "Quite a nuisance, you've been, one way and another."

"Pneumonia? ... What *happened*?"

"You fell in the weir. Don't you remember?"

"*Just* the kind of thing you were not supposed to do, if you recall," Eunice said tartly, taking the beaker from him. "But no doubt you had good reasons."

Now it began slowly to come back to him.

"I was in the mill – fighting Osmond – what happened? Did the floor give way?"

"*I* don't know, I'm sure!" exploded Mrs Tydings, who came in at that moment with an extra pillow. Her eyes snapped at Cosmo like sparks from green wood. She looked as if for two pins she'd have given him a good spanking. "You were the one who was supposed to be taking care! Getting up and skedaddling out in the middle of the night. Just you wait, my lad. Just you wait till you're out of that bed! I'll give you medicine!"

"I had to go, he was calling me ... What happened to the others?"

The very thought of that awful, hopeless fight began to make Cosmo feel weak and feverish. He lay back on his pillows.

"He's had enough talk for now," Eunice said. "You stay with him, Richard. Come on, Emma, you and I had better take ourselves off."

Cosmo was content to lie in silence with the comfort of his father's presence beside him. After a longish interval he asked,

"Dad?"

"Yes, Cosmo?"

"Are you in England to stay now?"

"Yes I am."

"That's good." He was silent again for a while. Then he said,

"Dad – were they ever found?"

"Yes. They were found," Richard answered, after a

moment's pause. "They were together, quite peacefully, as they must have died. On a little slope of hill. So we buried them there, and put up a stone with their names."

"It's an awfully long way from here," Cosmo muttered. He felt unspeakably sad.

"Not really ... "

"They did it to break the pattern," Cosmo said, half to himself. "It was a better way than that other horrible pair – " He thought of the hate-filled Osmond and his dreadful mother, ruthlessly intent to save her own son even at the cost of someone else's life. " – Dad – what's a *striga*?"

"I think it was some kind of witch," Richard answered. "A woman who could change herself into an owl and fly through closed doors."

"I wonder why she couldn't just kill me by her witch-craft? Maybe she had tried, and realized she couldn't. Because he was bound to fight me – "

"Are you getting delirious again?"

"No, no. – Where will you be living, Dad?"

"I'll do the same as you. Live in college during the week and come out here at weekends."

"Terrific ... " Holding his father's hand, Cosmo drifted off into thought or sleep. Then, suddenly coming to again, he asked, "When I fell in the weir – how did they know? It was the middle of the night?"

"Because of Lob. He roused Eunice. He was in a fearful state, barking and carrying on, quite frantic, wanted her to go outside. He more or less dragged her down there, she said. And there *you* were, bobbing around. Lob plunged in and hauled you to the edge, and between them he and Eunice managed to get you out. You owe Eunice quite a lot, one way and another. So do I."

"Good heavens," Cosmo said faintly. After a moment or

two he asked, "Where *is* Lob? I'd like to see the old fellow—"

Richard said, "Well—I'm afraid—that's not possible. You see, Lob was a very old dog. He was twenty. And pulling you out of the water was more of an effort than he'd made in a long time. It was more than he really had the strength for—"

"He's dead?"

"I'm afraid so. Yes."

"Oh, poor Eunice," said Cosmo. A long tremor went through him. He closed his eyes tightly and turned his head sideways on the pillow. "I've brought her nothing but trouble," he whispered, when the ache in his throat allowed him to speak.

"Oh, I wouldn't say that. No, I wouldn't say so."

Richard stood up.

"I have to go into Oxford now, to make various arrangements about my work. I'll see you later. Anything you want?"

"No, thanks, Father. I'm awfully glad you're here."

An hour or so later Eunice came in with a tray of soup and fruit.

"You can probably start getting up tomorrow, the doctor says. Just coming downstairs for a bit at a time."

"Eunice," he said. "I—I'm sorry about Lob."

He couldn't help it—the room dissolved round him in a wavering blur. Eunice sat down on his bed and they wrapped their arms round each other.

"Look, Cosmo," she said after a while. "He was an old, old dog. And rescuing people was what he was meant for. So, what a terrific way to go, don't you think? Much, much better than getting some horrid illness. We won't forget him in a hurry. But presently we might think of getting a puppy who'd be more company for you. – Now, try and eat your soup."

"Will you stay for a while? I'd like to talk to you."

"Yes, I was meaning to."

So, between mouthfuls of soup, Cosmo began to tell her about Con, and about Sim, and about Osmond and his wicked mother. She listened with the keenest interest.

"Do you think they were here all the time, Eunice?"

"Possibly so. And your coming here – in a rather tensed-up state – kind of fetched them out of limbo. I'd like to have seen Sim," she said. "He sounds nice. I think you ought to write all this down, Cosmo, while it's fresh in your memory. About Osmond and his mother – I suppose she couldn't help, poor woman, trying to help her son in the only way she knew, by studying black magic. Osmond was wrong about one thing though – he wasn't his mother's only son."

"How do you know that?" Cosmo asked, amazed.

"Richard and I have been looking at family records. Wait and I'll show you."

She went away and came back with a large, creased roll of paper, which, spread out, proved to be covered by a network of lines and names, like a spiderweb sagging from the top of the page. A family tree.

"Richard had this among his stuff – it goes back to thirteen hundred. He copied it out from the Dorchester records last time he was in England. Look here – Rosamond Curtoys and her son Osmond both died in the same year, 1768. But there was a younger son, Francis, born in 1762 and apparently not reared at home – there's a note about him here: 'Sent away as a babe to be brought up by Thos. Hendread, Yeoman. Returned in 1780 to claim his inheritance.' "

"I wonder why he was sent away?"

"Perhaps his mother took a dislike to him."

"Or his elder brother couldn't stand him ... I wouldn't like to have been Osmond's younger brother."

"It's curious about that pair, though," Eunice said. "Twenty years ago – one very dry summer, when your father and I were young – the river was extra-low, and they found two skeletons downstream from the weir, embedded in the clay bank. A man and a woman. They had forensic experts out from Oxford who said the bones were at least two hundred years old. And the woman was much older than the man."

"So that was what happened to them. I suppose you could say he died fighting." Cosmo shivered. "He was certainly no loss ... " Something cold shifted against his chest as he drew himself under the bedclothes; he put up a hand to feel it and found his George III penny, slung on the piece of binder-twine.

"We didn't like to take it off you," Eunice said, "because you kept clutching it and saying that it was your luck."

"It certainly was ... I'm sorry about the mill floor," he said, remembering that moment when he had seen the tip of Osmond's sword driving straight at his chest.

"Oh, it was in a shocking state. Ready to go. We're thinking of applying for a grant to restore it and turn it into a work-place for Richard; he'll need a studio or a lab out here. It's scheduled as a building of historic interest so you never know, we might be lucky. Finished? Okay, now have a good rest. There'll be lots to do when you start getting up ... "

She took the tray away.

Later that day Cosmo was allowed downstairs for a couple of hours, to sit in the sunny garden-room. He was glad when his father came back from Oxford; the big hearth, when he passed by, had seemed strangely bare and forlorn without the tousled black-and-white heap of Lob, stretched out on the warm stone.

"Do you feel up to seeing your friend Paul tomorrow?" Richard said. "I was talking to his father this afternoon. Norman said he could bring him out if you like; it's Saturday so there's no school."

"*School?* What's the date today?"

"May the fifth. You've missed a week's school already," Richard said. "You'd better hurry up and get back on your legs – you won't want to miss too much tennis."

"Gosh, no." Cosmo loved tennis. "Yes, I'd like to see Moley if he wants to come. He'll be disappointed if the furniture doesn't slide about, though."

"He'll just have to put up with his disappointment, then," Mrs Tydings said, coming in with a pot of tea. "The furniture's all settled down again, I'm glad to say. We don't want no more of *that* nonsense."

On the following day Professor Molesworth brought along Meredith as well as Moley. Cosmo was still not allowed out of doors – it was a cold, gusty May day – so he stayed in the garden-room while Moley showed Meredith round the farm and the island and the mill. They were reluctant to leave him at first, but Cosmo said, "Oh, go on. It's a shame not to show her while she's here."

When Meredith came back her eyes were shining. "Your look-out tree. Wow! What a place."

Richard had carefully vetted all the guard-rails the day before, and replaced the rotten one.

He had also, it seemed, told Professor Molesworth a certain amount about the family curse, and Professor Molesworth had told his son.

"You really are a lucky so-and-so, old Cosmic," said Moley enviously. "A family curse! That's a dickens of a lot better than having a stepmama and two dear little step-siblings. I'd swap, any day."

"I dunno, Moley," Meredith said. She looked thoughtful. "After all, you'll get away from your step-siblings in the end. But Cosmo will have the curse hanging over him to the end of his life. You'll *never* know, will you, Cosmo, whether it would be safe to marry and have children or not."

"No, I suppose I never shall – not for certain."

"Well, you'll just have to think of other things to do," Moley said robustly. "Children? Who wants them? Horrible little pests. I say, Cosmo, do show Meredith *Flatland*. I've been telling her about it."

Meredith was fascinated by *Flatland* and started reading it aloud: "'Down, down, down! Then a darkness, then a final all-consummating thunder-peal!' This sounds just like you, Cosmo, falling through the floor of the mill. – 'And when I came to myself, I was once more a common, creeping Square, in my Study at home, listening to the Peace-cry of my approaching Wife.' Oh, this is marvellous stuff! A common, creeping Square! Isn't that a perfect description of Mr Gabbitas."

Mrs Tydings brought them in their tea.

"Now you look a bit more like a human being, I *must* say," she remarked, fixing Cosmo with a sharp eye. "But don't you get over-excited now, with them squares and triangles."

"Flapjacks!" said Moley ecstatically. "Oh Mrs Tydings, you do know the way to a person's heart."

"We were wondering," said Meredith, after tea, "what you'd think about sharing a study with us next term, Cosmo?"

"Sharing a stu— ? Good heavens! But— won't you want to be sharing with Charley?" Cosmo asked Moley.

"He's leaving at the end of the term. His father's taken a job at the University of Santa Barbara and he's moving the family to California. So we thought— perhaps you— and us— and Sheil— "

"Sheil's awfully nice when you get to know her," Meredith said seriously.

"Well— yes. I'd like that. Very much." Cosmo thought, and said, "Who's going to share with poor old Bun?"

"Poor old Bun. He's not getting moved up. And it isn't because he doesn't take snuff," said Moley with an irrepressible chuckle. "Old Gab just told him he might be happier in the form below."

"I expect they'll be quite decent to him," Cosmo said, thinking of Tim and Frances.

And for himself he had a sudden flash of standing in Miss Gracie's line, buying four whipped-cream walnuts. "For you and your three friends, Cosmo?" "That's right, Miss Gracie."

"How were your holidays, Meredith?" he asked.

"Well, they were pretty horrible. Except for the last week. One thing: it's not so bad coming back to school."

"There's father," said Moley. Professor Molesworth was strolling over the lawn with Eunice and Richard. "I guess it's time to go. Thanks for a super tea, Mrs Tydings."

"You haven't eaten the half of it!" she scolded. "Wait while I put it into a bag for the pair of you to take back to school."

"See you soon, Cosmo. Hurry up and get well now!"

They said goodbye, he waved to them through the glass panels of the garden-room, and then the car drove off. Eunice and Richard turned and strolled over the meadow to the bridge, where they stood leaning on the rail, shoulder against shoulder, looking down at the water. Where I stood when I first saw Sim in the boat, Cosmo thought. And he remembered that other leavetaking, as Sim clanked off to join his uncle, valiantly singing:

> "Gallant are they
> Who now have gone
> With helmet and sword
> To Ascalon.
> If he be not
> In battle slain
> He will be a hero
> When he comes again."